LARRY'S FAMILIAR TALE

THE CROSSROADS KEEPER PREQUEL

SAMANTHA BLACKWOOD

CHARACTER LIST

MAIN

Jesse - A disillusioned witch who wants nothing more than to retire and play bingo. She's Larry's magical partner and the reluctant new manager of a supernatural scrapyard in the back of beyond.

Larry - Rottie-Pitt mix and Jesse's magical Familiar. Helps his stubborn new magical partner manage the scrapyard. His heroic actions end the book with a big surprise for everyone ... including Larry!

Carb - A ferrous demon with an unusual diet. Larry's new friend at the scrapyard.

Cerri - SBI Agent, Earth witch, priestess of the goddess Cerridwen, and all around badass. She and her crack team of SBI agents team up with Jesse and Larry to save the galaxy.

Cleo - Magical Familiar. She's a very bad kitty.

Litha - Wicked witch of **Salem**. She's a real piece of work.

Michael Malfisco - Magical mobster with no ethics and big plans. Grandson of Carlos Giotti, head of the local mage mob.

MINOR

Alcase - Long dead mage with a deadly hobby. He leaves a dangerous legacy his family line must protect … forever.

Carlos Giotti - Ruthless head of the Giotti magical crime family. Grandfather of Michael Malfisco and Anthony Manucci, the last two heirs standing. There are no good guys in this family.

Councilman Jenkins - Corrupt Witch Council Member. In bed with Litha, both professionally and personally.

Ed - Beaver Familiar. He's the first to offer Larry help when the chips are down.

Mary - SBI Agent and witch. An ancient potion master—and one of the best there is.

Midnight - A little black mama cat with a big job. She is the Felinus Universum and magical Familiar to Ted, the missing scrapyard manager.

Mort - Larry's caseworker at DEAF. A miserable demon with a vindictive streak a mile wide.

Risa - SBI Agent and Cerri's second-in-command. Powerful Water witch.

Sid the Raven - Magical Familiar. He's on Larry's side but can't really help much.

Ted - Missing scrapyard manager and descendant of Alcase. Along with his feline Familiar, Midnight, Ted is the keeper of a dangerous family legacy that could destroy the galaxy, if it falls into the wrong hands.

Violet - Brownie who cares for the manager's house at O'Malley's Supernatural Scrapyard. Extracts a promise from Larry for services rendered.

Sundry Other Bit Players

ABOUT THIS BOOK...
LARRY'S FAMILIAR TALE

A junkyard dog and his witch partner must save the galaxy...

After losing the battle for control of their coven to a wicked witch, snarky canine Familiar, Larry, and his grumpy witch partner, Jesse, are exiled to a supernatural scrapyard in the back of beyond.

Their only task is to keep an eye on things at the neglected scrapyard filled with piles of moldering magical machines ... until a mobster shows up demanding entry—or else.

Jesse and Larry are soon racing against the clock to find and protect a long-hidden magical machine before it falls into the wrong hands. The mobster mage who wants it plans to use the deadly astro-magical device to export his criminal syndicate to the stars. After all, crime pays, and there are so many other galaxies to exploit ... once this one is destroyed.

Will Jesse and Larry be successful in their fight to protect the scrapyard and its deadly device, or will one of them have to pay the ultimate price to save the galaxy?

This book is the prequel to my Crossroads Keeper series. Supernatural creatures of urban fantasy fill this modern tale filled with danger, humor ... and even a canine superhero.

Reader's Note: Larry's Familiar Tale is the prequel to my Crossroad's Keeper series. It tells Larry's backstory from his point of view. Other books in this series are written from his new magical partner's perspective, although Larry still has a lot to say … not surprisingly, lol.

Please visit my website for more information about this and other series:

www.samanathablackwoodnovelist.com

1

A FAMILIAR MEETING

"Look, I'm telling you, I don't think her death was natural. I'm sure that bitch witch killed her." Larry's fierce gaze swung around the covenstead's meeting room, blasting every Familiar present with fiery defiance.

Meows, growls, and chitters of protest filled the tense silence that followed his furious outburst. Larry shifted his weight, and the ornate wooden chair groaned in protest. The large room's assortment of delicate antique furniture was not meant for his massive Rottie-Pitt canine body.

Suppressing a frustrated growl, he cajoled the gathering of magical Familiars. "Come on guys, this isn't right, and you know it. Since our witch partners won't do it, then we Familiars have to investigate Mabel's death. We can't just let that bi— uh, Litha take over as High Priestess without making sure she's worthy of the role."

Larry woofed defiantly. "Look guys, I've been Mabel's Familiar for almost a century. We are ... were close, and she never once mentioned to me she had changed her mind about Jesse taking her place if anything happened to her." He growled, "Mabel would have told me."

The ancient grandmother clock against the wall chimed twice, its deep bong echoing throughout the dimly lit room. Orange flames in the fireplace reflected silver in the animal eyes of the gathered Familiars.

A sleek, ebony feline jumped onto the long conference table. Back arched in a sinuous stretch, she gave a disdainful meow. "Are we gonna listen to this mangey mutt's ranting for much longer? It's well after midnight, and I'd like to get back to my hunt. I've got better things to do than listen to Larry's mad conspiracy theories."

"He does have a point, though, Cleo," objected the midnight black raven perched on the mantle, feathers ruffling in the warm draft from the fire. "Mabel was only just over two hundred years old. She should have had a good century left in her, at least. Heck, I've known witches who made it almost to the half millennium mark. Maybe we should investigate our High Priestess's death. It's just a little too convenient that Litha was the only one with Mabel when she died—especially since she supposedly recently changed her mind and appointed Litha as her successor, instead of Jesse. We only have Litha's word for that, remember."

The raven's bright yellow eyes studied the cat on the table. "Cleo, as magical Familiar to Jesse—the coven member everyone expected to be the next High Priestess, I would have thought you'd be eager to discover if there was any foul play or shenanigans concerning the unexpected leadership succession change. Unless there's something you're not telling us?"

A tense silence filled the air at Sid's bold challenge. Larry's powerful muscles bunched under his sleek, dark fur as the surrounding Familiars gazed avidly between Sid and Cleo. He had done his best; it was up to others now either to support his request for an investigation or to deny it. To believe him or not.

Cleo broke the silence, snorting in derision and giving the raven a narrow-eyed glare. "Listen, Sid, I've been Jesse's

Familiar for almost a century. If anyone should know that she's not suitable to lead this coven, it would be me." She curled her lips in feline disgust. "Jesse just isn't High Priestess material, folks. Seems like Mabel finally realized that and appointed a better successor."

Voices rose in shocked protest at Cleo's denunciation of her long-time magical partner.

"Now hang on a minute, Cleo."

"Jesse's the smartest witch we have!"

"You can't believe that Mabel would—"

"Jesse's always been good to me—"

Larry closed his eyes and heaved a dejected sigh. Not enough voices protested Cleo's silkily persuasive words. Not nearly enough. Most of the Familiars ranged around the room kept their silence and avoided eye contact with each other. And with him. He had lost, despite support from a few valiant souls like Sid the Raven.

There would be no investigation of their late coven leader's untimely death. Litha would be sworn in as the new High Priestess on the next Full Moon ... in less than a week's time.

Goddess, help them all.

IT'S TOO LATE

Early morning light cast a golden glow over the pasture. Jesse reclined under the swaying branches of a massive willow tree whose deep roots anchored the earthen bank and extended into the stream below. A small waterfall murmured gently, helping to soothe Jesse's grieving soul. She had to accept the truth, whether or not she wanted to. Mabel was dead. Her High Priestess and best friend for almost a century had crossed into the Underworld, leaving Jesse and the rest of the coven confused, saddened, and at odds with each other. And worse.

Despite her best efforts, Jesse's thoughts kept returning to the horrible scene that had played out several days earlier, when Litha, a relatively new coven member, had returned from a walk in the woods with grave news. Mabel had always been an attentive listener; coven members regularly sought her out for advice, which was usually dispensed during a walk with their High Priestess on the coven's extensive grounds.

When Litha had walked out of the woods that day, she calmly told everyone that Mabel was dead, her body already absorbed back into Mother Earth. While the news of her friend's death had shocked and saddened Jesse, she had vowed to step into the High Priestess role for which Mabel had trained her. She would do it for the sake of the coven.

Sobs and wails of grief had echoed in the air, but Litha had remained strangely unmoved. Even now, Jesse could swear the woman's eyes had sparkled in sly triumph, but the expression had been fleeting. Instead, face grave with portent, Litha had raised her hands and called for silence.

Once everyone quieted, Litha had dropped a second bombshell. "Listen up, coven members. While our late coven leader's death is very sad, I think she may have been expecting it. You see, Mabel told me six months ago that she no longer thought Jesse the best fit to run the coven in the event of her death and that she needed to train a suitable successor."

Litha's next words had almost destroyed Jesse, and they were still reverberating through the coven days later. "The thing is, Mabel has been training me ever since then to take over as High Priestess, in the unfortunate event of her death."

Amid shocked gasps, and with everyone's not-as-surprised-as-they-should-have-been gazes pinned on her, Jesse had simply nodded and hurried away to mourn her friend and mentor. She had been avoiding her coven-mates ever since.

JESSE ABSENTLY RAN her fingers over the willow tree's leafy strands. *What did it really matter, anyway?* She mused sadly. In truth, she had always wondered at Mabel's wisdom in appointing her as successor all those years ago. Jesse knew she had never really fit in with the other coven members, most of whom kept her at a distance. While this social exclusion had made her an introvert, she had always faithfully performed her coven duties, despite private doubts about her fitness for the future leadership role for which Mabel insisted she was the best choice.

She sighed, wondering if Mabel had recently seen the error of her ways and decided to bypass her for another, more suitable coven member. But Litha? No, it surely couldn't be.

A faint breeze whispered through the willow fronds, the tree's soft, leafy strands whispering across her tear-stained cheeks. Jesse recalled her last private conversation with Mabel just over a week ago. They had been sitting in the dim light of the High Priestess's study sipping an excellent red wine from fancy crystal goblets—one of Mabel's few indulgences. A slight frown had wrinkled the coven leader's brow.

"What's the matter, Lady Mabel? You look worried. Is it the wine? Should I get you a fresh glass?" Jesse had asked her long-time friend and mentor.

Mabel had shaken her head and forced a smile. "Nothing's the matter, Jesse, dear. I'm fine. There's a situation with one of the coven members that is concerning me a little. But no matter. I'll handle it."

"If you tell me about it, maybe I can help," Jesse had replied, sipping her wine slowly, leaving space for Mabel to decide whether or not to share her worries.

"I think—no, I suspect ...." Mabel had started, before halting and rubbing her eyes with a sigh. "Listen, Jess, I would really rather not say too much until I'm absolutely sure. I'll tell you this much, though: someone's had their hand in the coven's coffers. That, I'm sure of. And there's, ah, a bit more to it than that, I suspect. But never mind all that for now." Mabel had then pointedly changed the subject.

Jesse fervently wished Mabel had been willing to share more about her suspicions during that last meeting. When Jesse had pressed for details, Mabel had simply shaken her head, telling Jesse she needed to confirm her suspicions before she shared them.

The breeze stiffened, blowing the willow tree's fronds into a merry dance. Jesse shivered, but not from the chill wind. She should have demanded Mabel give her answers. Now, it was too late. For everyone.

3

THE CONSPIRACY CAT

Larry gobbled down the last of his morning meal, then gave a satisfied belch before running his tongue around the bottom of the bowl to ensure he hadn't missed a single piece of kibble. No such luck, though. No more kibble.

And no more Mabel, Larry brooded sadly. He heaved a dejected sigh, ears flat against his massive head. This was one of the last meals he would eat at the High Priestess's house. In less than a week, it would be the Full Moon, when Litha would be sworn in as the coven's new High Priestess, and he'd be officially out of a job.

Even if Litha wanted him to stay on as the coven's High Familiar, which Larry highly doubted, there was no way he would agree. He couldn't work magic with a witch he despised … one he suspected of murdering Mabel, his magical partner and best friend.

That witch bitch would just have to bring her ancient toad Familiar with her when she took over as High Priestess. Burt wasn't the sharpest toad in the shed, or the most magical, but he'd do as High Familiar in a pinch.

The pantry door swung open, revealing Cleo's smug feline smile. "You'd better chow down now, mutt. You'll be out on your ear soon."

"Oh, stuff it, Cleo," Larry snarled at the cat. "What are you doing here, anyway? Shouldn't you be helping Jesse prepare for the Full Moon induction ritual? Even if she won't be the next High Priestess, as a coven member, she still has a role to play in the ritual."

Cleo's sinuous body slunk into the pantry, then she sprang onto a narrow shelf high above Larry's head. She casually licked her paw before running it over her glossy fur. "Jesse doesn't need my help anymore. Anyway, I'm too busy assisting my soon-to-be new magical partner get ready for the ritual."

Recently eaten kibble roiled in Larry's stomach, leaving him nauseous. Oh, no. "So ... Litha's asked you to be her High Familiar, has she?"

"Yep." Cleo's muzzle wrinkled in a self-satisfied grin.

"It figures," Larry muttered in disgust. "But what happens to Burt?"

Cleo's eyes gleamed with malice. "Burt will be retiring from the coven. Permanently. It's about time for that old toad to return to the Underworld so those losers at the Department of Eternal Animal Familiars can issue him a new body and assign him a new magical gig, don't you think?"

Larry schooled his features so the horror he felt didn't reflect on his face. "Litha plans to sacrifice Burt at the Full Moon ritual, doesn't she?" His heart hurt for the aged Familiar. The poor toad's physical death and his spirit's untimely arrival at DEAF for reassignment was cruel and unnecessary. That bitch.

Cleo balanced on the narrow shelf, then dove over Larry's head before landing on an even narrower shelf on the far wall. She gave Larry a haughty smile. "It's a High Priestess's prerogative to request a new High Familiar when she ascends to the role. You know that, dog breath."

Larry growled at the scheming cat. "Usually, it's just a personnel shuffle, Cleo—and you damn well know that. It's been centuries since a new High Priestess sacrificed her outgoing Familiar, instead of just reassigning them within the coven. Why can't she just let Burt find a new magical partner? Or assign him to Jesse? Since you're leaving her, she'll need a new Familiar—"

"Jesse already has a new Familiar," Cleo purred. "You."

"What?!" Larry barked in shock. "With Mabel ... uh, gone, I figured I'd be heading back to DEAF for a new assignment ... uh, after I take care of a few things." Larry wasn't about to tell Cleo of his plan to investigate Mabel's death. Even though the other Familiars refused to help, he was determined to discover the truth.

"You don't have a choice, I'm afraid," Cleo replied. The sleek feline stared coolly down at Larry and snickered. "Litha has already cleared your new Familiar assignment with your case worker at DEAF. You and Jesse are a magical team now. I warn you; she's not the easiest witch to work with. She's ... distant. Not too bright. A bit of a prude. Doesn't think the ends always justify the means ... if you know what I mean."

Larry suppressed the menacing growl that threatened to escape his muzzle. He'd be damned if he let Cleo see how her cruel, disloyal words about her former magical partner affected him. "Jesse is the smartest—and most powerful witch in this coven of magical misfits, Cleo. I'll be proud to partner with Jesse as her new Familiar."

Head held high, Larry stalked out of the pantry. He vowed to make sure he and Jesse developed a great personal and magical relationship. But first, he had to break the news to her that her long-time feline Familiar had deserted her for greener magical pastures. He didn't think Jesse would be too upset about it, though. She wasn't a cat person—even if said cat was her Familiar. And Cleo was SUCH a cat.

Once he explained things, Larry was sure Jesse would happily accept him as her new magical partner. He could then convince her to help him investigate Mabel's death. Once they uncovered the truth, they could sort out that bitch, Litha, and take back the coven's reins.

4

A NEW MAGICAL PARTNERSHIP

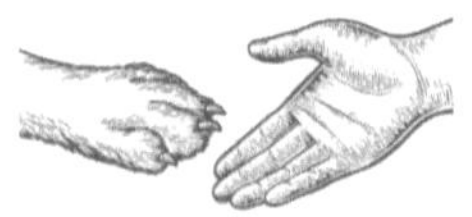

"Soooo, it doesn't bother you that Cleo has accepted a transfer?" Larry stood by Jesse's bed, studying his new magical partner through narrowed eyes. She was taking the news of Cleo's defection even better than he expected. Rather too well, in fact.

He wondered if her lack of reaction resulted from depression over Mabel's death, or from being unexpectedly denied her rightful leadership role in the coven. Probably a bit of both, he reasoned.

"Nope, I'm not disappointed in the least." The mound of pillows in which she had buried her head muffled Jesse's matter-of-fact statement. "Never was a cat person ... and Cleo was such a cat. I'm perfectly happy to be without a Familiar for the foreseeable future."

Larry sneezed to cover his snicker at Jesse's unknowing repetition of his own low opinion of Cleo ... and cats, in general. He heaved his bulk onto the bed and pawed away the pillows so he could observe Jesse's face when he shared the rest of his news.

"Um, I'm afraid there's more."

Jesse eyed Larry with raised brows, a flicker of interest lighting her gaze. "What? Don't tell me the Familiars voted to investigate Mabel's death at your meeting last night. I figured those losers would surely go along with Litha's plans to take over the coven, just like almost all the coven witch bitches have done."

"They're not all losers." Larry protested before tilting his head in consideration. "Just ... enough of them. The ones with the loudest voices."

"You lost the Familiar vote, then. That means there'll be no investigation into Mabel's death." Jesse's face fell in resignation.

"Well, no ... and yes. If you're willing to help," Larry said slowly. He brought his face closer to hers and widened his chocolate-brown eyes in entreaty.

Jesse studied him, then snorted a reluctant laugh. "Don't give me those big puppy-dog eyes, you little weasel. They may have worked on Mabel, but they darn sure won't work on me."

"How about if I throw in a head tilt and a raised paw?" Larry followed his words with the actions, then threw in a big, jowly, doggie grin for good measure.

Jesse's formerly surly expression softened; she pushed him away and sat up. "Oh, go on, then, you ginormous fur-ball. Spit it out. I'm listening." Lips twitching as she spoke, she struggled to contain a smile.

Pleased that he had lightened Jesse's mood—and got her face out of that mountain of pillows, Larry hoped his next words didn't bring back the dark thunderclouds that had figuratively surrounded his new magical partner when he first entered the room. "Two things, Jess. The first isn't negotiable, as I'm told it's already a done deal. The second is one I'm hoping you'll support, since you feel the same as me on the topic. At least I think you do."

"I'm all agog, you furry menace. Tell me, for the goddesses' sake!" Jesse made a 'gimme' gesture with her hands.

"Okay then, here goes." Larry sobered, then fixed apprehensive eyes on Jesse. "First of all, I'm now your magical Familiar. Apparently, Litha has some pull with the Witch Council. The Council requested the transfer from DEAF, who approved it without consulting me."

Larry realized his tone had grown annoyed and amended his statement. "Not that I mind being your magical partner, of course. I think we can work well together."

"Okay." Jesse's one-word response held no enthusiasm. Neither did it hold resentment.

"Okay? That's all you've got to say? That scheming bitch is moving pieces on the coven chessboard before she's even officially sworn in as High Priestess and 'okay' is all you can say?" A frustrated growl rumbled deep in Larry's massive chest.

Jesse patted the air and said, "Keep your socks on, you flea-bitten hound. I'm fine with you as a magical partner, so it doesn't matter to me it was Litha who arranged it. Although, I wonder about her motive." Her forehead wrinkled in thought. "What the flying fuck is she up to, I wonder?"

Larry curled his lips, long canines gleaming in the sunlight streaming through the window above the bed. "That brings me to item number two on the news list. I also want to know what Litha is up to ... and whether she—or anyone else—had anything to do with Mabel's death. Since the coven Familiars aren't willing to investigate, and your witchy coven-mates don't appear to have a brain cell or backbone between them, I'm thinking ... why don't we look into things? You and me?"

Various emotions flitted across Jesse's expressive face before surprise won out. "Us? But how? And what do we do with whatever we discover?" Her head drooped, and she sighed heavily before absently grabbing a pillow and hugging it to her chest. "No one's going to listen to us, anyway."

"Well, we can damn sure try," Larry responded. He shook his head, jowls and ears flapping. "I want to know what happened the day Mabel died, and I think you do, too. Her death wasn't natural, Jesse. I'm sure of it. I also highly doubt she suddenly changed her mind about who she wanted to take over the coven in the event of her death. Litha's only been with the coven for a few years and she's a magical lightweight—not to mention a complete bitch."

Larry placed a gentle paw on Jessi's arm and said, "You've been Mabel's chosen successor for over half a century. And you have more magic in your little toe than anyone else in the coven, including and especially Litha."

Jesse remained silent for so long that Larry worried he wouldn't gain her support in his investigative mission. When she finally spoke, her voice contained both hope and despair.

"I agree with you, Larry. We should honor Mabel's memory by doing what we can to right the wrongs we suspect that Litha and her supporters are doing to this coven. But I have to warn you, I'm not sure we'll be successful. I have a sinking feeling the rot goes deeper than we know."

She fingered the bedcovers, tracing the outline of the quilt's hand-sewn squares. "Mabel made me this quilt thirty years ago, you know," Jesse murmured. "She saw me admiring hers one day and told me right then she'd make me one. And she did. She always did what she said she would. And she always paid attention to people's needs and desires."

A lone tear tracked down Jesse's cheek. She ran her hands through her curly brown locks, which, even at one-hundred and thirty years old, were only lightly streaked with gray. Her normally pleasant, middle-aged face was a rictus of despair. "I realize now that I have been lax over the past few years, Larry. Maybe I let things the coven members did—or didn't do, slide when I shouldn't have. I didn't always listen and wasn't always the best assistant High Priestess to Mabel. Maybe that's why ...."

Larry's ears perked up. "Why what?"

Studying Larry intently, she reluctantly replied, "Well, a couple of weeks ago, when Mabel and I were having our monthly leadership meeting, she seemed troubled. I asked her what was wrong, but she wouldn't tell me. All she would say was that she suspected someone had their hands in the coven's coffers. Then she muttered there might be more to it, but she wouldn't tell me who she suspected ... or what the 'more' was."

Jesse's laugh was bitter, and it echoed in the cabin's small bedroom. "I should have pushed. Demanded that she tell me what she suspected and let me help resolve things. But I was so wrapped up in the small stuff: internal coven bickering, redecorating the altar, ordering magical supplies. Stupid stuff, it seems, in retrospect."

"What happened to Mabel is not your fault, Jesse," Larry protested. "We all get caught up in the day-to-day grind. Sometimes we overlook the big stuff going on around us because we're so busy taking care of the small stuff. And, as assistant to the High Priestess, the small stuff was your job."

The massive dog laid his head heavily on Jesse's knee and gusted a sigh. "It wasn't your fault ... but maybe it was mine. I warned Mabel about a month ago that I suspected Litha was up to something, but she told me not to worry. She said she was sorting things out. I should have forced the issue ... done something ... helped somehow."

Jesse, who had been unconsciously rubbing Larry's ears during his rant, paused her ministrations and patted Larry sharply on the head. "If it's not my fault, then it sure as hell isn't yours, dog-face. Did she tell you what she thought was going on? No. Even though you asked, many times, I assume." She gazed down at Larry inquiringly. When he looked away, she nodded and said, "I thought not."

"But—"

"No buts about it, you big mutt. Mabel refused to share her concerns with either of us, even though we asked her to. Several times. That's on her." Jesse resumed her rhythmic rubbing of Larry's soft ears. "We'll both just have to live with the fact that we knew something serious was bothering her, but we didn't press her hard enough for answers. We didn't trust our gut, and we didn't try nearly hard enough to verify that Mabel really had things under control. That's on us."

LARRY RELAXED into Jesse's ministrations, his eyes growing heavy with fatigue. He hadn't slept well since his magical partner's death. He yelped in surprise when Jesse suddenly grabbed his head firmly and brought her face close to his.

"Listen, you fathead," she growled. "You did your job. You warned your magical partner that you thought something was amiss ... more than once. She kept telling you she could handle it. That really is on her. Maybe you could have done something about it on your own, but more than likely not. Maybe you and I should have talked and tried to come up with a plan to help, but would it have made a difference?"

When Larry reluctantly shook his head, Jesse grinned down at him. "That's right, fur-face. It almost certainly wouldn't have made a difference. We both know Mabel was a stubborn old coot. She was responsible for her own destiny, Larry. We should always offer help and support to our friends, but they will only accept it when they are ready."

The painful burden on Larry's heart lightened, if only a little. "So, what you're saying is that nobody listens to anyone else, and that's not anyone's fault but their own, and that everyone is in charge of their own destiny."

"Something like that, you mouthy mutt," Jesse responded as she rolled off the bed and straightened her rumpled clothes.

Larry jumped off the bed and shook himself from head to rump, thick fur rippling over his muscular frame. He absolutely adored the huge Rottie-Pitt mix physical form he had managed to sweet-talk that temp caseworker at DEAF into assigning him for his present incarnation. He wanted to keep it as long as possible.

"Well then, Jess ... let's go be responsible for our own destiny. Time to investigate the hell out of that jumped-up hedge witch." Fixing his new magical partner with a gimlet eye, he added, "And, just for your information, I do not have fleas."

Jesse smothered a grin. "Maybe I should get you a flea collar."

"Don't you dare. You know Familiars don't get fleas." Larry gave Jesse a serious side-eye. "We're made of magic."

"There's always a first time," she snarked.

Their good-natured bickering followed the new magical duo as they left the room to prepare for their upcoming investigation.

UNCOVERING THE TRUTH

The following evening, Larry slunk away from a clandestine meeting half-way around the world, spirits buoyed by what he had just learned. If his informant's story was true, they had Litha bang to rights.

Apparently, the ethically challenged witch had tried this same takeover shit at her last coven, but the coven's High Priestess had gotten wind of it in time and taken immediate action. She had stripped Litha and her co-conspirators of their roles and kicked their asses out of the coven.

Larry frowned at the implications of what he had just discovered. He knew that Litha's Witch Council record was currently squeaky-clean. Someone on the Council must be in cahoots with Litha, because her record had been scrubbed ... and then embellished. When Litha and a few of her cronies had applied to join Mabel's coven several years ago, their records had appeared spotless.

Larry sighed as he loped through the darkness, considering what their investigation had turned up so far. He and Jesse had snuck into Mabel's empty house the night before and spent the night ransacking the coven's records, discovering within the faint trail of Litha's deceit.

Litha's Witch Council file contained several interesting discrepancies. Her coven application had not included a letter from her former High Priestess; instead, it had contained one from a prominent Witch Council member. That was odd, but not totally unheard of. Sometimes, High Priestesses and their assistants did not get along—too many witches in the kitchen, so to speak.

They had also discovered that Litha had a Familiar before Burt. Apparently, her previous Familiar had remained with her former coven when she left. That was highly unusual, and certainly something he and Jesse should investigate. Familiars usually stayed with their magical partners for life.

EVERYTHING THEY HAD LEARNED during their late-night study of the coven's records the night before had brought them thousands of miles away from their Salem covenstead—to the frigid northwest of England. They waited until the next evening, when all was quiet at the covenstead, and then traveled the ley lines to Carlisle, hometown of Litha's former coven, to see what more they could learn about Litha's unusual exit.

Fortunately, it had been a quick sixty-minute journey with only one short layover at a Crossroads near Stonehenge. Once in Carlisle, it hadn't taken Larry long to make contact with Litha's former Familiar and get the truth from him. If they left soon, he and Jesse would make it back to their covenstead before dawn ... if they didn't freeze to death first. *Brrrr.*

"Did he have any information?" Jesse's murmur, soft on the frigid night air, startled Larry from his introspection. He fought his way through the hedge until he reached Jesse's hiding place, snug up against the gnarled branches of an ancient hawthorn tree. She clutched her voluminous black cloak closed, shivering in the chilly night air.

"Yep," Larry whispered as he snuggled close to Jesse for warmth. "Litha's former Familiar, Dean the Dachshund, spilled the beans, and what he told me confirms our suspicions. Their coven's High Priestess discovered that Litha and her cronies were plotting a coven takeover."

A pang clutched at Larry's heart, but he ignored the pain of his own failure in not discovering the rot within their own coven until it was too late. He shook off his regret and explained his findings to Jesse. "Dean discovered Litha's nefarious plot and turned her and her co-conspirators in to coven leadership. Litha and her crew were out on their ears in less than a day. The High Priestess offered Dean the High Familiar spot, since the coven's current High Familiar had apparently been in on the plot, too. Dean accepted her offer and stayed."

He snorted and shook his head. "I get the feeling Dean would have stayed on with the coven in any position or begged DEAF for a new assignment. From what he told me, he and Litha had an extremely troubled magical partnership."

Jesse chuckled darkly. "Let me guess. Dean the Wiener Dog just wanted to do a good, honest magical job for the coven, while witch-bitch Litha wanted to remake the coven in her image through treachery and deceit."

"Yep. You nailed it," Larry replied. "And, in case you hadn't guessed, that's how Litha wound up with Burt. He lost his High Familiar role for being in league with Litha and her co-conspirators. He left with Litha and the others when the High Priestess gave them all the boot."

Jesse frowned thoughtfully. "I never did quite take to Burt. Thought it was a toad thing. I'm not a fan."

Larry snickered softly. "So, you don't like cats or toads. Any other animal Familiar forms don't you like?"

"You're just lucky I don't mind dogs," Jesse replied with a grin.

The two partners discussed their next steps as they made their way back to the Carlisle Crossroads for the long journey home.

They now had proof of Litha's previous dark deeds. But would it be enough to convince everyone she was repeating them in her new coven? Niggling doubts grew in the darkness of a cold English night half a world from home.

JUDGEMENT DAY

In the early light of dawn, and exhausted from their return journey through the ley lines, the pair stumbled into Jesse's cottage, then collapsed on her ancient, but comfortable couch. As their weary eyes closed, a sharp tap sounded on the window behind them.

Tempted to ignore it, Larry burrowed under the soft blanket covering his end of the long couch. Jesse snored softly, having already sunk into sleep.

Tap, tap, tap. Caw. Tap, tap. "Hey guys, let me in. It's Sid. We need to talk." Tap, tap. "Come on, guys! Wakey, wakey! The early bird gets the worm and all that!"

Sid's continued efforts finally produced results. Jesse groaned, then reluctantly sat up. She reached behind the couch and unlocked the window latch. The glossy black raven demanding entry quickly hopped onto the windowsill, then flew into the room before landing expertly on a large piece of driftwood decorating the coffee table.

Sid cocked his head, his yellow eyes bright with warning. "You guys are in so much trouble. That blabbermouth cat, Cleo, discovered you two have been snooping around. She told Litha you've been trying to find dirt on her."

Jesse rolled her eyes, then threw Larry a narrow-eyed glare. "See? I told you that bitch would find out. Now what?"

Larry's stomach sunk at Sid's words. He ignored Jesse's question and asked Sid to explain. "What's the scoop, bud? What's Litha planning to do about our investigation?"

Sid ruffled his feathers in annoyance, worry in his avian eyes. "She's called an emergency meeting of the coven and requested a Council member attend in case there's a need for, ah, judgement."

"Well, shit." Jesse blurted. She met Larry's troubled gaze, seeking support. "We've got the goods on her, though, right? We know exactly what she's been up to. She's even done this before. We have proof. Witnesses. All we need to do is get her former High Priestess and Familiar here to testify—"

Agitated, Sid bounced up and down on the driftwood. "Those of us with any sense already know that Litha is bad news, and some of us also suspect she had a hand in Mabel's death. But there's more of them—idiots, that is, than there are of us. Most people just don't want to see what's right in front of them. They'd prefer to ignore the warning signs and just go with the flow, especially if they think the outcome doesn't directly affect them."

Larry's ears drooped and he rumbled a growl. "I hear you, Sid. But we have to at least try. When is the emergency meeting?"

"That's what I'm trying to tell you guys! It's already started. You both need to get your butts over to the covenstead if you want to have any chance of a say in the proceedings against you."

Larry's eyed widened in dismay. "What?! How can Litha just call a special session without informing the full coven ... which, at this point, still includes us? And who calls a coven meeting for this time of the morning? That bitch!" Larry's lip curled in a snarl, his sharp canines on full display.

Jesse and Larry shared a horrified look, then launched themselves off the couch and raced out the cottage door. Sid flew over their heads, beating them to the covenstead by a feather.

ACCUSING eyes scrutinized Larry and Jesse as they hurried into the coven meeting room. The large space was stuffed to bursting, with every coven member and Familiar in attendance, despite the early hour. The atmosphere buzzed with unpleasant anticipation.

Litha sat at the head of the conference table, a smug smile on her beautiful face and ice in her eyes. "So glad you two could make it. Better late than never, right?"

"Now wait just a minute," Jesse sputtered. "We came as soon as we heard about the meeting—"

A deep, masculine voice cut off Jesse's angry protest. "Please take a seat, Goodwitch Jesse. Larry, please sit next to her. We have a lot to discuss this morning, and most of it concerns you two."

Larry's heart sank. The presence of Councilman Jenkins confirmed their worst fears. The councilman's signature was on the Witch Council's letter of recommendation for Litha—and the man had even roused himself before dawn and travelled the leys to attend this early morning meeting to support his beautiful witch protégé. A haughty, if bored expression blanketed the man's sharp-edged face, but his dark brown eyes sparked with angry malice.

"*That's my chair*," mused Jesse sadly. She mind-spoke her distressed thoughts to Larry. "*That bastard is sitting in my chair ... the one at Mabel's right hand ... and Litha seems to have already claimed the chair at the head of the table reserved for the High Priestess.*" Jesse sunk into a seat at the far end of the table, as far from the evil witch bitch as she could get.

Larry's rumbling voice mind-spoke his reply. "*Don't let them see you sweat, Jess. No matter what happens, girlfriend, don't let any of these yahoos see you sweat. You're better than that.*"

Jesse rallied at Larry's encouraging words. She raised her head and met Litha's arrogant gaze head on. "You've been scheming to take over this coven since you got here a couple years ago, haven't you?"

When Litha didn't respond to her accusation, Jesse gave the woman a sly smile. "Larry and I have been doing a little investigating into your background, Litha. We have witnesses who will testify that you tried to do the exact same thing in your previous coven and that the High Priestess kicked your ass out when she discovered what you were up to."

Jesse pointed an accusing finger at Litha. "This time, though, you didn't take any chances. You killed Lady Mabel, our much-loved High Priestess, before she revealed your treachery. And now you seek to discredit me—her rightful successor—so you can take over this coven for yourself."

Into the shocked silence Jesse's accusation caused, Larry woofed, then jumped onto the table and padded down its length before stopping directly in front of the corrupt councilman. He growled down at the man, "You're in this up to your neck, aren't you, Jenkins? You're the one who scrubbed Litha's Witch Council record and signed the letter of recommendation she used to gain entry to our coven."

Murmurs of disbelief and anger susurrated around the vast room, echoing from the high ceiling, giving the impression of thousands of voices rising in sibilant disagreement.

Councilman Jenkins jumped to his feet, his voice cutting through the tense air. "Quiet! Everyone needs to sit down and shut up. NOW!" Once a tense silence returned, he divided his glare between Larry and Jesse. "Do either of you have any evidence here today to back up your wild allegations? Witnesses? Documents? No? I thought not." His thin lips curved in a wintry smile, and he nodded once returned to his seat.

The councilman's emphasis on the words 'here today' made it clear to Larry that the arrogant fool had no interest in waiting for either evidence or witnesses to be produced.

Larry slid a glance towards Litha, who reclined proudly in the High Priestess's chair, with Cleo sitting smugly on her lap. While Litha tried to hide her glee at the councilman's stern words, she couldn't quite pull it off. What a scheming bitch.

Purposely avoiding Litha's triumphant gaze, Larry mind-spoke to Jesse. *"I'm afraid the fix is in, Jess. These two assholes are in this together. We don't have a chance. Besides, do you really want to stay in a coven that would allow this to happen without a fight? Especially one soon to be headed by the wicked witch of Salem?"*

Jesse's defeated voice sounded in Larry's mind. *"No, I don't want to stay here. Especially not now that Mabel's gone. I thought ... I don't know. I guess I hoped others would see through Litha's scheme, or that we'd have time to gather evidence and witnesses against her. But she's been one step ahead of us the whole way, hasn't she? And my erstwhile Familiar, that devious cat, has been helping her the whole time."* Jesse snorted in disgust and glared at Cleo. *"I've been so blind."*

"You and me both, Jesse. You and me both. There's not a lot we can do about it now, though. The best choice we have is to resign before they fire us," Larry mind-spoke his reply, schooling his expression so his despair didn't show. *"Never let them see you sweat."*

Jesse nodded decisively and jumped to her feet. She

slammed her hand on the table, interrupting the proceedings —and her inevitable excommunication. "I hereby renounce my membership in this coven. I quit. You win, Litha ... this time. But there will be a next time, I assure you." Jesse's defiant words rang out in the room, the certainty of her pronouncement a portent of judgement to come.

Larry padded back down the table before jumping off and pressing himself into Jesse's side. He gazed in disgust at the silent observers and growled, "I'm so done with this festival of fools. I quit, too. The lot of you will get what you deserve ... and you'll soon discover it's not what you think ... or want."

"Oh, knock off the dramatics, you two." Litha's sharp command left no doubt of her triumph. "And it's too late for either of you to resign, since you have already been cast out. The coven has already voted, and you have been found guilty of grave disloyalty to this coven and its members. Black marks will be entered in both your Witch Council records, for sure. No other coven will have you."

Dryly, Jesse replied. "Unless we cheat and have our record expunged, like you did after the last time you tried this shit, you bitch. And just how did you get that letter of recommendation from the esteemed Councilman Jenkins here? Hmmm? And how did you secure his cooperation in this farce of a trial? Slept your way to the top, did you?"

"That's enough!" Face red with outrage, the councilman in question shouted. "You will show respect in this chamber, Jesse! I expect nothing less, nor does High Priestess Litha."

"So, Jesse's right, then. Touched a nerve, did she?" Larry's snarky reply enraged the furious councilman even further. Larry watched with interest; if the man's face got any redder, his head might just pop off and fly around the room.

There was no point in mincing words, Larry realized. The fix was definitely in; he and Jesse would be lucky to escape today's judgement with nothing worse than a transfer to some crappy job in a god-awful magical backwater. *Sigh.*

Councilman Jenkins passed judgement; his tedious words falling into the room's utter silence like drops of bitter water into a tainted pond, oily ripples widening as they spread.

"Jesse Taylor and Larry Familiar, the Witch Council has accepted the petition put forward by the newly appointed High Priestess of the Salem City Coven and approved by a majority of coven members to remove you both from coven membership. Under Section 3.6-5, subsection b, d, and f of the Witch Council Code ...."

Larry tuned out the councilman's droning pronouncement. While he had attended this type of hearing many times before, he had never been the one directly affected by the Witch Council's judgements. Now he knew why the defendants always bore a look of dazed confusion.

Schooling his face into impassivity, Larry stifled a sigh, then flicked a glance at Jesse, who sat stone-faced, hands clasped loosely in her lap. He mind-spoke words of encouragement. *"Jesse, keep it together. Don't show them anything. We'll get through this together."*

Jesse's eyes narrowed; it was the only outward sign she heard Larry's mind-spoken words, which she answered with a sharp reply. *"Of course, we'll get through this, you big dufus. I know that. After all, I've attended plenty of these hearings before over the past century or so."* Her lips thinned. *"Just never one where I was the one under judgement."*

"Right there with ya," Larry replied soberly.

The councilman's prolonged statement was nothing but a monotonous background noise to the mind-conversation between the two defendants. "And under Section 18.5-21, related charges, specifications and magical reassignments ...."

Reassignments ... Larry's ears perked up, and he tuned back into the councilman's words. It was time to find out how bad their next magical assignment would be.

THE BACK OF BEYOND

"Motherfucker. Shit. Damn. That brass-balled bitch! I'll turn her into a freaking toad one day, don't you doubt me." Jesse's profanity-laden tirade continued as she threw clothes haphazardly into the open suitcase on the bed. "I'm gonna curse her boobs to sag to her ankles and give her wrinkles the size of the Grand Canyon."

Larry reclined on a pile of pillows at the head of Jesse's bed, listening to her angry dialog with half an ear. She had been alternately cursing Litha to the bowels of the Underworld and spewing lewd comments about the sexual favors Litha must have granted the crooked councilman to get such a quick trial and favorable verdict ... and such a completely crappy reassignment for them.

"I hope her hoo-ha freezes shut while that prick's dick—"

"Jesse. Jesse? JESSE!" Larry barked loudly to add emphasis to his words.

"What?!" Jesse grouched, abandoning her packing efforts and sinking onto the bed with a groan.

Larry eyed his new magical partner speculatively, hoping

she had worked off enough of her ire to discuss their reassign-ment like a reasonable witch.

"Maybe we should talk about our next assignment, Jess. I mean, it sounds like a pretty cushy gig even if it is in some tiny backwater town in Connecticut. All we gotta to do is manage a supernatural scrapyard full of old, broken-down magical machinery ... how much work can it really be?"

An ominous sense of foreboding filled Larry. *I've probably jinxed us,* he brooded.

JESSE SIGHED and ran her fingers in a familiar pattern over the hand-sewn squares of the quilt Mabel had made for her decades ago. They both knew that Mabel's recent death had precipitated this whole cluster-fuck. And, no matter what Larry said, Jesse still believed she bore some blame for the current mess by missing the warning signs of deceit and treachery within the coven and by not demanding answers from Mabel about her suspicions.

Larry was right about their next assignment, although calling Bridgeport a tiny backwater town might be stretching things a bit. However, while the city had a substantial human population, its supernatural population was infinitesimal. Other than the nearly defunct magical scrapyard to which they had been assigned, there were less than a half a dozen other struggling supernatural businesses in town.

Their new assignment really was a in magical backwater—certainly nothing like the very witchy city of Salem they were being forced to leave behind.

Jesse's shoulders slumped in defeat. "What's there to talk about, Larry? We're being sent to the magical equivalent of Siberia."

She smoothed the quilt Mabel had made for her, unconsciously seeking what comfort it offered. "Sid told me after the coven meeting that he heard the last scrapyard manager disappeared about a month ago ... and apparently no even one noticed until a few days ago."

Huffing a frustrated sigh, she added, "He probably packed his bags and took off for greener pastures. Or maybe he died of boredom, and we'll find his body buried under a crap-ton of metal scraps when we get there."

~

WITH A DETERMINED NOD, Jesse stood and resumed her packing. "Anyway, this whole coven takeover thing makes no difference to me anymore. I'm done being a 'good witch'. In fact, I'm done being any kind of witch. I'm retiring. I'll go and live at this stupid scrapyard because I've got nowhere else to go, but don't count on me for any help running it."

Larry only just held back a massive eye roll. He couldn't avoid an annoyed sneeze, though. Then he sneezed again, for good measure.

"Hey! Don't you get snot all over Mabel's—my quilt, you disgusting creature."

Just to be contrary, Larry wiped his nose on the quilt. "Listen, Jesse, I know it sucks that you lost your High Priestess and best friend. Don't forget, she was my magical partner, so I'm grieving her loss, too."

He huffed a sigh and gave his new magical partner a sympathetic side-eye. "And it really sucks that Litha pulled off a coven coup right under our noses. But there's nothing we can do about it right now. If we just give up, then she wins. And dammit, I'm not about to let her win. That witch bitch may have won this battle, but the war isn't over. She'll trip up. We'll keep digging and try to find a sympathetic Council member to hear our case." Larry cocked his head in consideration. "Or at least one that she's not sleeping with."

Jesse snorted. "Might be hard to do, though. That bitch has probably slept her way through most of the male members on the Witch Council."

"Let's not be sexist now, Jesse. She's probably slept with one or two of the female Council members, as well." Larry curled his lips in a doggie smile, his massive pink tongue hanging over sharp white teeth. "Not that there's anything at all wrong with that, of course ... other than the whole corrupt 'sex for influence' aspect, that is."

The atmosphere in the room lightened. Jesse's guffaws bounced off the bedroom's low ceiling while Larry's canine chuckle rumbled in accompaniment.

Once their laughter had abated, Jesse reluctantly amended her plans. "Alright, I'll just semi-retire, then. I'll do what's needed to help you run the magical side of things at the scrapyard, but you know that's not gonna involve much more than keeping an eye on things and making sure no one steals any of that useless crap. I'll still have a ton of time to pursue my non-magical interests."

A thoughtful expression settled on her face. "I've always wanted to play Bingo. And I hear they have Greek diners in Connecticut. I love diner food; plus, those places usually have Early Bird specials for seniors."

Larry's jaw dropped in disbelief. "Bingo? Senior specials? You're not an old lady, Jesse! You're not even human! As a witch, you're no more than middle-aged, and you damn well know it. You've got a good couple centuries left. And at your age, your magic is at its most powerful."

"I told you, fur-face ... I'm semi-retiring. Those prime of life magical years can blow. I've given almost a century of my life to helping Mabel run this coven. It's my turn now to do things I enjoy—and I like a lot of human things. I've just never had the time to do most of them. Besides, you know I can magic myself to look whatever age I want." Jesse stroked her curly, light brown hair with a sly smile. "Do you think I should go with a silver-purple color? Or maybe white with a bluish tint? Glasses? Cane or walker? Oooh, how about one of those nifty disability scooters?"

Larry couldn't help dissolving into amused laughter. Jesse joined him.

Once their mutual mirth abated, Larry grumbled, "You're being ridiculous, Jesse, and you know it."

Jesse sat up, hand on her side, which had a stitch in it from laughing so hard. She protested Larry's assertion. "No, I'm not being ridiculous, and no, I don't know it."

"Yes, you are." Larry replied, sniffing disdainfully.

"No, I'm really not. Semi-retired witch here, remember?"

Jesse and Larry's bickering only abated once they reached the Salem Crossroads. They would use the ley lines to travel to their new assignment, since Jesse no longer had a car. The old Ford Taurus she had been driving for the last decade belonged to the coven; she'd had to turn the keys in before they left the covenstead. *Sigh.*

"Ready, Jesse?" Larry padded onto the ley station platform.

"Ready as I'll ever be, you mangey mutt. Let's blow this popsicle stand."

"No one says that anymore, Jesse. That's so old-fashioned."

Jesse waved at her altered appearance. Before they left the covenstead, she had used magic to age herself and now sported deep wrinkles, short, silvery-blue hair, and a shapeless housedress dotted with purple pansies. Thick-lensed purple glasses hung from a beaded chain around her withered neck. "Well, I'm an old lady now, bud, so if the orthopedic shoe fits ...."

Larry rolled his eyes and snorted a laugh. "Let's go, you old crone."

Jesse grinned and followed Larry off the platform and into the ley line.

8

HOME, SWEET HOME

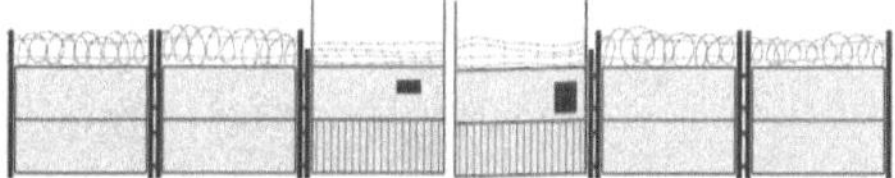

Several hours later, a taxi deposited Larry and Jesse outside the rusted metal gates of O'Malley's Supernatural Scrapyard, their reluctant new magical assignment. They had traveled via ley lines to the New Haven Crossroads, then taken a human taxi the rest of the way, since Bridgeport was too supernaturally insignificant to have its own Crossroads. The taxi puttered off as the tired duo examined the closed chain-link gates leading to their new home.

A small metal sign hung crookedly from the tall chain-link fence, announcing in peeling white paint that they had arrived at O'Malley's Scrapyard. The 'supernatural' part had been left off the sign for obvious reasons. The supernatural scrapyard and its soon-to-be new inhabitants were just a tiny magical dot in a very large human city and both really needed to stay under the radar.

A smaller, but equally tattered, sign hung above an old-fashioned brass bell-pull; it instructed visitors to Ring Bell for Service. A massive chain, and an equally large lock, secured the scrapyard's gates. Another decrepit notice hung directly above the lock: Closed.

The run-down, abandoned look of the place threatened to douse Larry's determination to tackle their new assignment with at least a modicum of enthusiasm. "I say we ring the bell and see if we actually get any service, like the sign says," he growled.

"No one's here, you ding dong. We're the ones who are supposed to be answering that damn bell, now that the former manager's done a runner." Jesse eyed the lock speculatively. "Give me a hand, Larry. Let's get this lock open. I'm exhausted and I need to put my feet up. These damned orthopedic shoes are killing me."

Larry stifled a sigh before padding to Jesse's side. He raised his magic and directed it towards Jesse's hand, which rested lightly on his back. Jesse combined her magic with Larry's and touched the lock with her index finger. The lock quickly clicked open, newly applied oil shining on its hasp. Once Jesse removed the chain, the gate opened with a small push, rolling smoothly on well-greased tracks.

Hmmm. Larry realized someone must still be caring for the place, despite its abandoned air. As they walked through the gates and glimpsed the scrapyard beyond, their jaws dropped in amazement. Or horror. Or a little bit of both.

Enormous, rusting mountains of magical metal scrap filled the vast acreage. A mammoth crusher hulked at the far end of the huge, open space, its cab sitting easily two stories above the dirty, cracked concrete. Several forklifts with flaking orange paint huddled under a three-sided metal shed.

Weeds pushed up through the cracked concrete forecourt and climbed the chain-link fencing. Spindly trees struggled to survive in planters made of old truck tires dotted haphazardly throughout the almost apocalyptic landscape. Above a large wooden shed near the gate hung a sign identifying the dilapidated building as the office.

"Fuuuuuuck," Jesse murmured.

"Ditto," Larry muttered, nodding absently in agreement as his gaze swept the enormous space. There had to be living quarters somewhere on the property. The Witch Council better not be expecting them to bunk down in the scrapyard's office.

Then his gaze sharpened, and he poked Jesse with his nose before tilting his head towards a small, nicely maintained gingerbread style cottage partially hidden by a row of over-grown bushes. "The house looks nice, though, Jess. Cared for. Pretty little garden. Lots of bushes around the perimeter to pee on."

Jesse huffed a sigh of relief, then rolled her suitcase across the decaying forecourt, toward the one welcoming structure in the nightmare landscape that was O'Malley's Supernatural Scrapyard. "Let's go check out our new home, fur-face."

PREDICTABLY, they found a house key hidden under a clay flowerpot adorning the front steps. The brass key slid into the lock with ease. Again, Larry sensed someone must still be caring for the place, even though the last manager had been missing for over a month and, judging by the unholy mess littering the scrapyard, wasn't the tidy type.

As Jesse pushed open the door, the sweet scent of beeswax and lavender wafted out. Larry padded quickly through the opening and twirled around in the hallway, eyes and ears wide open. No one about that he could sense, but someone had recently been in the house and had cleaned it from top to bottom. There wasn't a speck of dust anywhere.

"I think we've got a House Brownie," Jesse murmured with satisfaction. "No other creature cares for a home quite as well as a Brownie."

She made a show of wiping her finger along the top of an elegant side table that perched on spindly legs under a rather magnificent antique mirror and smiled in delight. "Sir or Madam Brownie, we appreciate and applaud your most excellent housekeeping skills. I've seen none better in my very long time on this earth. I do hope you'll stay on now that the former occupant of this home has gone. We newcomers would be lost without you, as would this lovely home."

Larry knew Jesse's flowery praise was designed to placate the Brownie and encourage her—or him to stay on. He hoped it worked. He had already discovered that Jesse's housekeeping skills were lackadaisical, at best. His were non-existent.

After a thorough inspection of their new home, every room as spotless as the last, the exhausted friends collapsed on the large, overstuffed couch in the living room.

"I'm starving hungry," Jesse said. "How about you? Want some of your delicious kibble for dinner?"

"I could do with a kibble appetizer, but what's actually for dinner?" Larry replied, licking his chops in anticipation.

Jesse heaved herself off the couch and headed into the kitchen. "There's a bunch of takeout menus on the fridge. Let's see what looks good and order delivery."

Just over an hour later, Larry finished the last of his kibble and belched. Out of habit, his tongue made one last pass around the metal bowl. Nope. All gone.

"Can you please stop clattering that thing around the kitchen floor? I'll have to get a rubber mat for it, so it doesn't make such a racket on these tiles." Jesse griped absently as she popped the last piece of a truly delicious pizza into her mouth and wiped her greasy hands on a napkin. "Boy, they sure don't make pizza like this in Salem," she moaned.

"They don't make real pizza at all in Massachusetts, or in most states, for that matter," Larry griped. "What they do make is some kind of tomato pie with a thick, chewy crust, bland canned sauce, and waaaay too much cheese." He cocked his head, lips curling in distaste. "What passes for pizza in most of the country looks and tastes like New-York-style pizza and Chicago pizza got together and had a nasty pizza-baby."

He snickered at his own joke, then stopped when a delicious memory surfaced. "Oh wait, remember that trip we took to San Antonio last year, when the coven was thinking of applying to move there, if the opportunity arose? We ate at that place run by a vampire who's a retired mobster from New York. What's his name? Oh yeah! Vinnie." Larry snickered again. "Vinnie the Vampire."

Jesse grinned and nodded. "That's right! Vinnie's pizza is definitely the closest thing to real pizza you can get in that Italian American food desert, otherwise known as Texas." She covered her mouth and gave a satisfied belched. "Oh, boy ... this pizza almost makes it worth coming to this goddess-forsaken hell-scape that calls itself a supernatural scrapyard."

Larry hopped up on the chair next to Jesse and gave her puppy-dog eyes. "Can I have another pizza bone? I'm still hungry."

Jesse broke a piece of crust off the remnants in the pizza box and passed it to Larry, who took it daintily before gobbling it in one go. No chewing required. *Yum.* He licked his jowls and wondered if he could get away with the rest of the crusts in the box before Jesse stopped him.

From the warning look in her eyes, Larry realized Jesse had already sussed out his pizza crust theft plan. He abandoned it and instead said, "Well, if great pizza is the only thing required to get you to accept this place as our new home, I'm sure we can work something out. The Giardi's Pizzeria menu is on the fridge and their number is on the house phone's speed dial."

Silence reigned as the duo considered a life filled with

excellent pizza. There had to be an upside to their current situation. Good food worked.

"Besides, wherever you are ... there you are." Larry stated firmly, giving Jesse a wide doggie grin.

"Thanks for that, fur-face," Jesse snarked. "It makes everything sooo much better."

Larry fought not to roll his eyes and snap a reply, but couldn't stop a low, grumbling growl. "I thought we hammered this out on the journey down here, Jesse. If we work hard, we'll soon get this scrapyard in shape, then we should be able to run it in our sleep. That'll give you time to play at being a human senior citizen and me time to continue our investigation into what happened to Mabel."

Jesse scrambled out of her chair, almost tipping it over, then grabbed the pizza box and stuffed it in the trash can. "Not that crap about the investigation again. Can't you just leave it? It's over and done with. I'm semi-retired now, remember? No more magical leadership roles. No more witch politics. I'd suggest you leave the past in the past, as well, Larry."

She sniffed and furtively rubbed her eyes. "I'm freaking done with it all. I'm telling you, I'm gonna buy some crappy costume jewelry to go with my old lady look and join the senior center down the street."

"That huge one we passed on our way here?" Larry asked, eyes wide in disbelief. "But it's run by the Catholic Church! In case you've forgotten—you're a witch, Jess. I'm not real sure you won't go up in flames if you step foot on church grounds."

"Don't be ridiculous," Jesse protested. "As you darn well know, during the Burning Times, many practicing witches hid themselves in plain sight in church pews." She grinned wickedly. "Some of them even became nuns—and none of them ever burst into flames when entering a church."

Larry gave his new magical partner a wan smile, but centuries-old grief shadowed his eyes. "Yeah, but a fair few of those witches, plus a whole bunch of innocent humans, had themselves lit on fire in village squares during the Burning Times. Just be careful, Jess. I know humans don't burn witches at the stake anymore, but still ... it's a good idea to keep a low profile."

"I'm just an elderly, frail senior citizen who wants to play Bingo and socialize," Jesse croaked, mimicking an old-lady voice. "I'm as human as they get," she added, then burst out laughing.

Despite his misgivings, Larry couldn't help but laugh with her.

9

NIGHT WATCH

After dinner, Jesse gave an eye-watering yawn. "I'm exhausted. I'm going to bed early. We can check out the scrapyard in the morning. Or not. Maybe not. Let's go find a real Greek diner and have a big, delicious breakfast instead." Happily muttering about eggs over easy, hash browns, and strong diner coffee, Jesse toddled off to bed.

Larry shook his head in dismissal of Jesse's cavalier attitude regarding their new assignment. He was determined he would not fail another magical partner by not staying on top of things. If Jesse wasn't yet ready to tackle their new magical duties, he'd just have to pick up the slack.

The kitchen door featured a cat flap. After several valiant efforts to squeeze his giant Rottweiler Pitt-bull mix body through an opening meant for an obviously skinny, and probably mangey cat, Larry admitted defeat. Sighing in resignation, he called up a small amount of magic—just enough to unlock the door and open it.

His jet-black fur blended into the darkness as he investigated the scrapyard's mountains of abandoned magical machinery. He raised his head and inhaled deeply, nostrils quivering in the cool night air. Yep, his first impression when they had entered the scrapyard was correct. He and Jesse weren't the only ones living within the razor-wire-topped chain-link fence. There was at least one other supernatural creature occupying the scrapyard, besides the Brownie, of course. Larry again thanked the goddess for that Fae blessing.

Larry picked up his paws, one after the other, and shook them. His other impression from when they arrived was that there was more magic in this place than there should be. A whole lot more. It buzzed in the air and rumbled under his paws. For a place that was supposed to house nothing more than a crap-ton of deactivated magical scrap, most of its former use long spelled away, the powerful magical energy emanating from somewhere amongst the mountains of rusty relics concerned Larry a great deal.

A SKITTERING SOUND, claws on metal, startled Larry. He listened intently, then raced towards the sound. Better to discover and dominate all scrapyard inhabitants, supernatural and otherwise, right from the start. As he rounded the corner of the office shed, paws kicking up dust with his speed, something small and hard bounced painfully off his side. Skidding to a stop, he took cover behind the shed, away from the direction of fire.

After several tense minutes, when no other sounds broke the nighttime silence, Larry peered around the corner and examined the area beyond with a frown. A large metal screw lay gleaming dully in the moonlight. Seconds later, another screw flew at his head, and he ducked back behind the wall. The screw hit the wall where his head had been moments ago with enough force to dent the wood.

"Alright, you numbskull. Just stop with the throwing shit, or I'll come out there and make you stop. And I promise you won't like how I'll do it," Larry growled, putting enough magical energy into his words to make most supernatural creatures cower in fear. He wasn't one of the oldest and most powerful Familiars ever to exist for nothing.

Instead of immediate surrender, a maniacal laugh greeted Larry's threat. "But first, you'd have to catch me, Familiar. And I know this scrapyard like the back of my claw. You're huge. And slow. I can hear you coming from a mile away. Smell you, too. When's the last time you had a bath?"

Claws tinking on metal, followed by a small avalanche of metal parts clinking down the side of the closest scrap mountain, alerted Larry to the location of the crazy supernatural creature who dared to defy him.

Now he was pissed. He raised magic until his body glowed golden in the dim moonlight, then gave himself a magical push behind his powerful back legs, which propelled his body halfway up the metal slope in a single bound.

"Woah, dog breath! You'll bring this whole mound tumbling down if you're not careful," warned a low, growly voice. A toddler-sized, green-skinned creature climbed out from behind a piece of machinery and squatted a few feet away from Larry's landing spot.

The creature's muscles were tensed for flight, but his oddly shaped face bore an affable grin. "Howdy, there pardner. I hear you and that old woman you arrived with are from the Western states. Where's your horse?"

"You heard wrong." Larry ground his teeth and prepared to spring. "We're from Massachusetts, not the Midwest, you dipstick. Anyway, it's the twenty-first century; nobody travels by horse anymore."

The creature's eyes grew dreamy. "They do in the Underworld. Enormous animals the horses there are, too, with fiery eyes and sharp teeth. Sharp enough to eat metal, but the creatures just chomp on boring old grass. Oh, and the occasional idiot demon stupid enough to piss them off."

A lightbulb came on in Larry's head. He grinned in surprise and asked, "You're a ferrous demon, aren't you? If I remember right here on Earth, they call your kind gremlins. You guys eat metal for dinner, right?"

"For breakfast and lunch, too. Yum!" The strange, but mostly harmless little demon crowed as he rubbed his round green belly. "A scrapyard's a great place for us ferrous demons. There's an endless supply of tasty metal, all just piled up and waiting to be eaten."

Larry gazed doubtfully at the massive mounds of formerly magical metal waste stretching almost as far as the eye could see. "You can't be very hungry then, because this place looks untouched."

"Hey! Enough with the insults, fur-for-brains! I'm a picky eater. And not very big. It doesn't take much to fill me up, so don't worry about the scrapyard going out of business anytime soon for lack of magical metal pieces and parts." The little ferrous demon belched. "Just hope you're not needing any carburetors. I polished the last of those off ages ago."

The creature settled on his haunches; his compact body now flanked by long, skinny legs. He wore a ratty loincloth tied around his waist, and a necklace made up of various small pieces of metal rested on his hairless chest. He gave a small head-bob, then grinned widely at Larry and said, "Name's Carb, by the way. Nice 'ta meet ya'."

Larry relaxed slightly, but kept his magic up, not yet convinced he could trust the weird little guy. "I'm Larry. My magical partner is Jesse. She's not really old; she's a witch. The old lady act is a disguise."

"Oh. Who's she hiding from?"

"Life," Larry muttered dismally. "She's hiding from life."

"Well, she's come to the right place, then. Nothing much

ever happens here," Carb replied. After a moment's hesitation, he tilted his head and added, "Well, not until recently."

Larry's ears perked. "What happened recently? Do you know anything about the missing scrapyard manager?"

"Oh, that," Carb muttered, his attention focused on a large, still-shiny screw near his feet. Quick as lightning, he snatched up the screw and popped it in his mouth, razor-sharp teeth crunching away. "Yum. Can't resist screws. They're sorta like potato chips ... one's never enough."

Resisting an overwhelming urge to bite the little green creature, Larry repeated his earlier question. "Do you know what happened to the last manager?"

"Sure do. About a month ago, I was relaxing in one a' them big bushes near the gate and munching on some screws when a couple of guys drove up in a van, got out, then rang the bell. When Ted responded, they asked him to open the gates. One of 'em was dressed all important-like—even had on a jacket that said SBI on the back in big white letters. The official-looking guy said he was from the Supernatural Bureau of Investigation. He told Ted—that's the scrapyard manager—that a broken magical machine the SBI had just confiscated was on a truck heading this way, and that it might be too big for the gates."

Carb snorted derisively and added, "Like that would happen. Those gates are twenty feet wide."

When Carb's attention returned to the scrap metal at his feet, Larry reined in his temper and prompted him, "What happened next?"

"Ted the Dummy left the magical protection of the wards and walked right up to their van—that's what happened next," Carb replied. "Then two big guys jumped out, threw a blanket over him, and bundled him into the back of the van. The other two hopped in front and the van drove off in a hurry." Carb popped another screw into his mouth and chewed. "Haven't seen Ted since."

The low-level concern Larry had already felt about the missing scrapyard manager bloomed. Something was very wrong. "What happened to Ted's Familiar? I scented a magical cat when we first got here."

"Midnight? Oh, she took off after the van. Haven't seen her since, either," Carb replied. He poured a handful of small nails into his open mouth and chewed noisily.

Thoroughly annoyed by the ferrous demon's cavalier attitude to the missing manager and his Familiar, Larry barked at him, "And you didn't think to tell anyone about this at the time? The Witch Council thinks Ted quit with no notice."

"I did tell someone!" The little demon protested. "About a week after Ted went missing, some geezer from the Witch Council showed up. Tall dude, skinny. Smarmy, superior attitude. He and his buddy showed up one night and tried several times to get through the gate wards, with no success. When I challenged them, the stuck-up one told me he was from the Witch Council and was looking for the manager. He asked if I'd seen Ted lately."

Carb snorted and shook his head. "The smug bastard told me they were on official business and insisted I open the wards and let them inside immediately. I asked to see his Witch Council ID and asked if he could prove his visit was official. When the jerk-wad refused to show me his ID, or proof he had legitimate business at the scrapyard, I told him and his friend to sod off—after telling them about Ted's disappearance. I figured the Council would eventually send someone to investigate, but no one came … until you two showed up today."

Waving his hands lin exasperation, the demon protested. "What more could I do? As a ferrous demon, I'm way too magnetic to use modern electronics without frying them, so I couldn't call or text anyone, and I couldn't leave the scrapyard unattended, or another ferrous demon would have moved in on my turf and I'd have lost it. I know I look big and strong to you, but I'm small for my species. I'm very lucky to have found this place, and I'm not risking losing it for anyone."

Larry gave Carb a tired smile. "Okay, simmer down, bud. Sounds like you did what you could." He rubbed a paw over his nose in thought, then fur rose along his back when he realized the import of the little ferrous demon's words.

"I think I know who the guy is from the Witch Council ... the one you saw who tried like hell to gain access to the scrapyard. His name is Jenkins; he fits your description and is as corrupt as they come. But who was his accomplice on the night they tried to break or bully their way in, I wonder? And what the hell are they after here in the scrapyard?"

"Couldn't get a good look at the councilman's partner," Carb replied. "His break in buddy was wearing a dark sweatshirt with the hood up, but I'm pretty sure it was a woman." He fingered a large screw but didn't pick it up; he was getting full.

LARRY CLOSED his eyes and exhaled slowly. Litha. Jenkins' female accomplice had to be her. Those two were definitely up to something ... but why would Jenkins send him and Jesse to work at the scrapyard if he and Litha wanted access to it themselves? Wouldn't it make more sense to leave the place unstaffed?

Then it hit him. Neither the corrupt councilman nor Litha considered them a threat to their nefarious plans. What better way for Councilman Jenkins to gain access through the scrapyard's powerful wards than informing the Witch Council of the scrapyard manager's disappearance, then convincing them to send replacements he recommended?

The asshole had probably told the Council that he just so happened to know of a disgraced witch and her Familiar partner who were perfect for the job.

Once the Witch Council appointed Jesse and Larry as Ted's official replacements, ward access for them was immediately conferred. All Councilman Jenkins and his witch bitch partner in crime had to do after that was show up at the scrapyard after their arrival and demand Jesse or Larry let them in.

Still, their actions made little sense: after the despicable way Jenkins and Litha had treated them, what made the scheming pair think either would willingly grant ward access to their new home. And why had they tried to break in several weeks ago? Something about the whole messy situation still escaped Larry.

"Well, if you're done talking, I'm off. Places to go and things to do and all that." Carb rose to his full three-foot height, his stick-thin legs appearing too weak to support his thick body.

"A couple more things before you go, bud," Larry said as he quickly sorted through the questions tumbling around in his mind. "Has anyone else attempted to gain access to the scrapyard, other than the councilman and his companion?"

Carb was already nodding in the affirmative. "Those big dudes who kidnapped Ted have been back almost every night since. They've tested the entire perimeter, but the fools have gotten nothing but a bunch of powerful magical shocks and a few nasty cuts from the razor wire, for their efforts."

With a pleased smirk, he added, "I'll say one thing for Ted. He damn sure knows how to set some powerful wards. They have barely weakened at all since he's been gone."

Which could mean only one thing, Larry knew. If the wards were still unusually strong, the scrapyard manager was still alive ... and he was almost certainly being tortured by whoever kidnapped him to gain his cooperation. The unsettling feeling he'd had since he first stepped through the scrapyard gates grew, gnawing at Larry's stomach.

"What about the important-looking guy you mentioned

seeing with the goons when they kidnapped Ted?" Larry asked. "You said he had on an SBI jacket, but—"

"But there's no way he was SBI," interrupted Carb with a snort. "Yeah, the supernatural police tend to be more the 'handcuffs and perp walks', than 'blankets over the head and kidnapping in the dark' types, don't they?"

The little demon crossed his skinny arms and eyed Larry thoughtfully. "In my humble opinion, you've got two sets of bad guys trying to gain access to this place. Maybe they're working together. Maybe not."

He nodded decisively and made an offer Larry couldn't refuse. "Listen, I'm nocturnal, so I can continue to keep an eye out at night. I'll let you know if either bunch of bad guys shows up again."

"Oh, I'm sure they'll be back, Carb. Whatever it is they're looking for must be hidden here in the scrapyard. Which brings me to my last question." Larry fixed the small demon with a stern glare. "What the bloody HELL are they after, Carb? You must know. You told me you know this damn scrapyard like the back of your claw."

After shrugging and examining said claw, Carb replied, "Beats me. I've only been here a couple years. Ted has been here for more than half a century. I'm assuming he knows what the bad guys are after, since it's likely he hid whatever it is here in the first place."

The demon eyed a pile of junk near his feet, then stooped to pick up a handful of screws. "I'll save these for later when I get peckish. If you got no more questions, I'll get back to my nightly rounds."

"Just one more thing," Larry asked. "Don't you sense the crazy amount of magical energy wafting around this place? I felt it as soon as I passed through the gates. There's gotta be a magical item of great power hidden here somewhere. And I don't think it's broken at all." Larry raised his head and scented the air, trying to determine from which direction the insidiously heavy magic emanated.

"Of course, I can sense the mega-magical energy, you dufus," Carb exclaimed. "What—you think I'm stupid? I felt it as soon as I moved in. When a friend first told me about this place, he mentioned that the last ferrous demon who lived here had up and left for no reason, so I beat feet over here and took over."

Carb's pointed green nose crinkled in thought, and he shrugged. "I'm not positive the extra strong magic is why the last demon left, though. Maybe he went to live with a girlfriend or he's on the run from the supernatural po-po." He shrugged philosophically and added, "There's a ton of really great eating metal here, and nobody bothers me, so I put up with the magical buzz."

Larry studied the ferrous demon thoughtfully, wondering if his new buddy was a bit dim, or just willfully blind to the truth. "You do realize that your ferrous demon compatriots, and most other supernaturals, avoid this place because of the massive amount of powerful—and almost certainly dangerous, magical energy here, don't you?"

Carb bellowed a hearty guffaw. "Oh, come on, now, I'm no dummy. 'Course, I know there's something seriously magical hereabouts. I'm just not inclined to ask too many questions about it ... or look for it. What I don't know can't hurt me, right?"

Larry shook his head and sighed. Here was another person who wouldn't listen to reason or ask for help. Someone with no sense of self-preservation. Mabel's stubborn face floated in his mind's eye. Grief threatened, and he whined a low protest before shaking off his sadness and refocusing on the here and now.

Fixing the ferrous demon with a stern glare, Larry told him, "Listen to me, Carb—keep your eyes and ears open. You're in charge of the Night Watch. Let me know right away if anyone comes snooping around. And for the goddesses' sake, be careful. Whatever's hidden here has already gotten at least one person kidnapped. I fear ...."

Larry didn't know what he feared, but he couldn't shake an ominous foreboding. This job would not be the easy, boring, cushy assignment that either he or Jesse had hoped. *Sigh.*

10

A WHITE HATTED CAT

Shadows of darkness slipped across the rusting mountains of scrap as clouds scudded across the night sky above. The massive piles of metal shifted, their insides creaking and tinking, as if they had a life of their own. After leaving Carb on night patrol, Larry shivered and hurried through the scrapyard, eager to get back to the light and warmth of the cottage.

The tall metal gate across the main entrance was firmly shut and locked, Larry noted as he passed it. Good. When a rusty, desperate meow wafted through the night air, Larry paused and listened. The sound had come from just outside the scrapyard, to one side of the gate.

"Who's there?" Larry's sharp query met silence. He padded over and shoved his muzzle against the chain-link fence, sniffing deeply, nose wrinkling at the acrid scent of cat. "I said, who's there? Name yourself."

This time, a testy meow answered his gruff query. Then a sarcastic, feline voice entered Larry's mind. "If you don't know by now that I'm a cat, then you aren't much of a canine, are you, dog breath?" After a disgusted sneeze, the cat spoke aloud. "I mean, I smelled your canine butt coming from a mile away."

"You still haven't answered my question, cat. Who are you?" Larry asked suspiciously, refusing to respond to the feisty feline's taunting insults. He focused his gaze through the chain-link fence and scanned the wide driveway. Larry suspected he knew the answer to his question, but wanted to hear it from the cat's mouth, so to speak.

A grumbly purr sounded, followed quickly by half a dozen smaller, high-pitched meows. The overgrown brush just outside and to the left of the gate rustled and a small black cat crept out from its leafy interior. The cat gave a pained meow, then limped across the driveway until it faced Larry through the fence.

"Hello, my name is Midnight," the cat explained. "I'm Familiar to Ted, the mage who runs ... ran this scrapyard. Some bad guys kidnapped him about a moon ago. I'm injured, and I have kittens with me. I need you to open the gate and let us in."

Larry nodded, then hesitated, wondering where the key to the gate's lock was kept. Jesse had used magic to lock up once they entered the scrapyard.

Midnight misinterpreted his hesitation and gave an impressive eye roll. "Okay, fur-face, since you're going to make me beg. Please open the gate and help me get my kittens inside. Nowwww-meowwww."

"Keep your fur on, cat. I'm new here. I just need to figure out where the key for this lock is kept or use some magic to open it if I can't find the damn thing. Plus, I want a little back up present when I open the gate ... in case there's any bad guys out there." Larry left out the part about wanting backup in case the cat was lying.

"Ak-ak-ak-ak." The cat chittered a feline laugh, but it ended in a pained groan. "The moronic mages surveilling this place are currently dealing with a pissed-off passel of ginormous rats with their tails tied together. Both the rat-pack and the mages are scurrying around near the back gate. We need to hurry before the fools realize the rats are merely a diversion, though."

"Let me get the key. I think it might be in the office."

"There's no need for the key." Nose in the air, Midnight emitted a screeching feline yowl. "Carb? Carb! Get your scaly green ass over here. I need some help, and this junkyard dog is clueless."

Larry squinted, his ears ringing from Midnight's cry. "Could you be any louder, cat? I'm sure the evil mages on the other side of the scrapyard didn't catch every word. Just most of them."

Carb materialized, seemingly out of thin air. "Midnight? Thank goddess, you're back! But ... where are your kittens? Surely, you've had them by now, considering how pregnant you were last time I saw you." The little demon pressed his face worriedly against the fence. "Are the kittens okay? You're injured, girl. I can smell blood."

"I've got a few injuries, but they're healing. And my kittens are just fine, Carb. Thanks for asking." Faint meows sounded within the heavy brush near the fence line, confirming the truth of Midnight's words.

She limped across the driveway toward her frightened kittens, then stopped and pointed a paw at the fence behind the brush. "There's a loose piece of fencing back there. I tried to push it aside and squeeze through, but as you can tell, I'm not at my best right now. Can you guys help?"

The rusted chain-link fence screeched when Carb shifted it to one side. The little demon urged, "Come on, Midnight. Hurry up and get the kits inside the fence—and the wards. Those idiot mages are surely headed this way."

The demon began pulling the wriggling, spitting balls of fluff through the gap in the fence and then quickly pressed Larry into service. "Grab 'em by the scruff, Larry. We need to hurry!"

Midnight gave whispered instructions. "Please take the kits into the office, guys. I'll build my nursery in there, where it's safe and warm."

As Larry and Carb hurriedly pulled the kittens through the gap in the fence, several angry voices sounded from the driveway.

"Damn rats! Who the heck tied their tails together? And how the hell did they catch 'em all in the first place?"

"You all right Will? That huge one gave you a big ol' bite."

"Yeah, I'm good. Too bad he got away before I could bite him back."

Just as the mages came into view, Midnight squeezed through the narrow opening in the fence, the last struggling kitten in her mouth. She mind-spoke, *"Leave the fence like it is. The gap is hidden from view. Plus, those birdbrain mages can't get through the wards—even if they could squeeze their fat asses through the opening."*

Larry snickered as he carried his last furry charge into the office. "You're alright, for a cat, Midnight."

"And you're alright, for a dog, Larry," she replied dryly.

ONCE THE LAST of the kittens dozed off, snug in their newly created nest under the desk, Midnight turned a serious gaze on Larry and Carb. "We need to talk, guys."

"First, let me check out your wounds, Midnight," Larry said as he padded toward the office's back door. "Come outside into the moonlight; it's bright enough out there and we won't disturb the kits."

After a token protest, Midnight accompanied Larry out back, where the bulk of the shed blocked them from view of anyone near the front gate. With only minor hisses and some mumbled profanity, she submitted to Larry's magical healing ministrations.

"There you go, Midnight. Sorry I had to re-break the leg. It had set badly," Larry said a short while later. He sat heavily, slightly dizzy and panting after using so much magic to heal the injured cat. "At least you aren't bleeding anymore. All the skin's healed over, but you'll need to take it easy on that back leg for a while. That was a bad break."

Despite herself, Midnight purred a sigh of relief. The pain of her injuries had subsided to nothing more than a dull ache. "Thank you, Larry. But you really didn't have to waste so much of your magical talents on me. I'd have gotten through it on my own."

Carb squatted next to Midnight, eyeing her critically. "Oh, drop the tough cat act, Midnight. Larry did you a favor. Plus, we need you feeling better so you can tell us what happened the night those goons kidnapped Ted, and you ran after the van ... and what's been going on with you guys since then."

Midnight huffed, then abruptly sat and began grooming her matted fur. "Sorry, guys, I groom when I'm upset. A hell of a lot happened that night, Carb, and even more since. I'll fill you both in. But first, tell me what's been going on here while Ted and I have been gone."

Larry quickly explained that the Witch Council thought Ted had just walked off the job. He explained about his and Jesse's reassignment to the scrapyard and filled her in on events to date.

Midnight snorted in disgust. She had groomed herself for the whole of Larry's report, but stopped when he finished, her fur now neat and gleaming from her ministrations. "Okay, now I'm beyond being upset. Ted's a good manager. And dedicated. He would never have just walked off the job. Besides, he'd never have left behind ...."

When she hesitated, Larry finished her sentence. "Yeah, he

never would have left behind ... whatever the hell piece of infernal magical equipment he's been hiding in this scrapyard." Head tilted, ears up, Larry eyed Midnight questioningly. "Spill, cat."

"Yeah, about that," Midnight drawled, her lips curled in a smug feline grin. "You haven't actually found it yet, have you? I can tell it's still here—and well hidden and warded, thank the goddess."

Larry gave Midnight a reproachful glare and growled, "Whatever the hell it is, it's caused a whole bunch of havoc— and got Ted kidnapped. You had better fill us in so we can sort out this absolute crap-fest."

"And save the galaxy, at the same time," Midnight replied softly, her green eyes glowing gold in the light from an errant moonbeam.

Larry stared at Midnight in shock. "Save the galaxy? What the hell are you talking about, cat?"

Midnight's emerald-green eyes shone with both old knowledge and new worry. "Yep, I said save the galaxy, and I meant it. You both need to know what's at stake here, so I'll explain. Listen up, guys."

As Midnight relayed her incredible tale, Larry's muzzle dropped open in amazement and Carb's impossibly large eyes grew even larger.

"Here's the scoop ... just over a month ago, a couple of mages started sniffing around outside the scrapyard. Ted caught one and questioned him. He learned the mages worked for some big mobster mage who was looking for a powerful magical machine. The mage didn't know where his boss heard about the machine, though, or how he discovered it might be hidden in the scrapyard. After getting all the information he could from the guy, Ted let him go ... after turning him into a rat, of course, so he couldn't report back to his boss."

Midnight's needle-sharp teeth gleamed in the moonlight as she smiled. "I had some fun with him before I ended things." She grinned at Larry's horrified expression. "No, I didn't kill the mage-rat, Larry. Just chased him off."

"Okayyyy. That's good," Larry replied, giving Midnight a wary side-eye.

She snickered and added, "The little guy didn't go far, though. He's one of the rats whose tails I twisted into a knot tonight."

Despite himself, Larry barked a laugh. A rusty chuffing sound came from Carb; the ferrous demon was laughing as well. The atmosphere lightened a bit but immediately tensed again when the duo heard the rest of Midnight's report.

Midnight told them that the mage mobster's goons had grown in number and boldness after the mage-rat incident. At first, they had come to the gate and asked nicely for admittance. When that didn't work, they resorted to threats. When Ted refused all their requests, they attempted to force their way into the scrapyard during their almost nightly raids. For weeks, Ted had worked tirelessly to strengthen the wards, successfully keeping the mages at bay ... until that last day.

Midnight sighed deeply, then rubbed her ears with her paws. She shrugged and gazed sadly at her rapt audience. "You guys know what happened next, right?"

Carb nodded in confirmation. "Yep, we know about Ted getting kidnapped and you jumping on the van before it drove away." The little demon's head dipped in shame. "I saw the whole thing from my hiding place, and I didn't help."

"There's nothing you could have done, Carb. I'm glad you stayed here at the scrapyard and kept an eye on things for us," Midnight assured him.

She rubbed her head against the demon's skinny legs. "I

reached the van before it got too far away. Then I climbed the damn thing and clung to the roof for miles. I only jumped off when we reached the end of the road by the old marina." She winced and added, "That's when I broke my leg."

"Way to go, Midnight!" Carb exclaimed in admiration, then he sobered. "That explains the broken leg, girlfriend, but how did you get all those other injuries? You looked like hell when you got here, before Larry worked his healing magic on you."

Midnight aimed an irritated glare at her demon friend. "Gee, thanks, Carb. Just what a girl cat wants to hear."

"Well, you did," Carb declared with a shrug.

"Being a homeless cat in a rough part of Bridgeport isn't easy, you know—especially when you're pregnant. The local cats thought I was trying to move in on their territory. I had to fight for my right to be there. But I needed to stay around the old marina to see if I could find out what happened to Ted and help him, if I could."

"Well, what did happen to Ted?" Larry asked. He hesitated, then continued. "Uh, he's still alive, right? Do you know where the bad guys are keeping him? You mentioned the old marina. Has Ted told his captors anything..."

"Yes, Ted is still alive, but he's in terrible shape," Midnight replied with a sad meow. "He's being kept near the old marina, on a boat moored to the dock near the old Cartwright Factory."

She chuffed derisively. "And no, Ted hasn't told the bad guys anything. He would die first." Her head hung low. "And he just might, if they hurt him much more. That's why I came back here. I need your help to free him."

Puzzled, Larry asked, "But how did you know we would be here? When you left the scrapyard last month, the only one left here was Carb."

Midnight explained that Ted had been able to communicate with her via mind-speak, as long as she stayed close to the old marina where he was being held. "Ted's no dummy. And he's very good with wards, so he's been sending what energy he can to keep the ones around the scrapyard strong. He knows the bad guys haven't yet breached them. There's an alert on the wards to let Ted know if anyone with good intent approaches them, so he knew the second you guys arrived. I headed this way as soon as he told me you were here."

"But why didn't he just send you to the Witch Council weeks ago to alert them to what's been going on? Oh, wait—" Larry's eyes rounded in understanding.

Midnight nodded. "Yep, I see you've realized the answer to that question. A Witch Council member has been helping the bad guys with Ted's ... uh, interrogation." She meowed sadly. "Since there's a traitor on the Council, we don't know who to trust."

Larry's heart sank; he already knew the traitor's identity. "Councilman Jenkins."

Regarding him curiously, Midnight nodded. "Yes, it's Councilman Jenkins. How did you know?"

Larry shook his head, jowls flapping. "Long story. Suffice it to say, we know Councilman Jenkins has his sticky fingers all over this situation. And I'm pretty sure Litha, the extremely evil new High Priestess of my former coven, is involved as well. I'm not sure if she and Jenkins are completely in league with the bad guys who kidnapped your partner, or if they are playing along and have their own plans for whatever magical thingy that's hidden here. In either case, we've got to stop them all."

"And get my partner, Ted, back. Alive."

"And get Ted back," Larry promised. Internally, he winced. Here he was, making promises he didn't know how to fulfill. But that's what friends were for, right? Midnight and her partner needed their help. He vowed to get involved this time and not ignore the danger creeping along under the surface of things. Poor Mabel. Larry's tail drooped.

CARB'S IMPATIENT growl cut into Larry's despondent musings. "So, tell us, Midnight ... what exactly does Ted have buried in this scrapyard that the bad guys are so hot to get their mitts on? And how did he come by it?"

Midnight studied both Carb and Larry somberly. When she finally spoke, her words carried great magical power. "What I'm about to tell you both is highly confidential. I need a life oath from each of you that you won't speak of it ever again once the danger is over."

"A life oath?! That means we'll die if we ever mention what you're about to tell us!" Larry sputtered; eyes wide as he stared at Midnight in dismay.

Her grave expression and intent gaze informed Larry that Midnight wouldn't budge on this issue. It was a life oath or no information. Carb and Larry shared a long, anxious look, then both nodded simultaneously and turned determined gazes back to Midnight.

Larry spoke for both of them. "If we're going to help you save the damned galaxy, we need to know what we're saving it from. Tell us everything, cat."

There was a tense moment of silence, during which Midnight studied them and took stock of their commitment. Once satisfied, she administered the life oath, which took very little time, considering the grave consequences it imposed. Then she told them everything.

"Alright guys, here goes ... the magical device hidden in the scrapyard is called the Universum. That's the Latin word for Cosmos. Ted's ancestor created it centuries ago, during the Enlightenment, when many scientists, both mundane and magical, were theorizing about life, the universe, and everything."

She snorted in disgust. "Knowledge is a good thing, if

pursued for the betterment of society. But when knowledge is used in the pursuit of power, and you mix in an unscrupulous astro-mage and a crap-ton of powerful dark magic, well, you get a device that can destroy the galaxy. The Universum."

Larry gulped, eyes wide in horrified wonder. "Why on earth would anyone create such a thing? After all, wouldn't they be just at risk if it was ... uh, used?"

Midnight settled herself more comfortably on her haunches and continued her explanation. "It's a long story, so settle in, boys. In answer to the first question: that fool created the Universum just because he could. Alcase's keen interest in physics and astronomy brought him into contact with Sir Isaac Newton, who took the younger man under his wing. Over the following decade, Alcase had a front-row seat as Newton developed his theories concerning celestial mechanics and universal gravitation. The seeds of the Universum germinated during Alcase's time with Newton."

Larry's muzzle dropped open in shock. "Are you saying that Sir Isaac Newton helped Alcase create the Universum?"

With a quick shake of her head, Midnight restored Larry's opinion of the famous seventeenth-century mage. Larry had never met him, personally, but he'd heard good things from those who had. There must be more to the story. He fixed Midnight with an eager, inquisitive gaze. "So then, what happened?"

"Unfortunately, Alcase never had the same moral standards as Newton," Midnight replied with a disgusted snort. "He always had to push the ethical envelope. The bastard took Newton's theories, combined them with those of other eminent scientist mages of the time, added in a whole shitload of dark magic, and created the Universum. Unlike his contemporaries, Alcase didn't want to just theorize about the vastness of the cosmos. He wanted to see it ... in person. That's what the Universum is designed to do—bend time and space, allowing its user to physically travel pretty much anywhere in the cosmos within seconds."

Midnight's forehead wrinkled, and her lips curled in disdain. "Alcase was simultaneously brilliant, evil ... and very, very foolish. Fortunately, once he finished creating the Universum, at least he was smart enough to test the infernal thing before using it. He was a member of the Royal Society, as well as the Mage Guild."

She eyed her listeners doubtfully and assumed a lecturing air. "As you may or may not know, the best philosophers and scientists are usually powerful mages, as well—a fact that the mages of the time intelligently kept under their hats during the Enlightenment." A shadow of darkness tinged Midnight's gaze. "Remember, not everyone was enlightened back then ... the more regressive members of the populace were still busy burning witches and other magical beings during that dark time."

After a moment of silence, during which the trio paid sad tribute to the many lives, both magical and mundane, lost during the Burning Times, Larry prompted Midnight to continue her tale. "The Universum test? What happened?"

"Alcase used his contacts at the Royal Society and the Mage Guild to gather a team of mages to observe his experiment. Obviously, he left out the bit about the crapload of dark magic he'd used to create his astro-magical invention."

Midnight paused, her eyes dark in horrified remembrance. "When Alcase started to chant the spell to activate the Universum, the whole world wobbled, then the very air shimmered and thinned ... and thankfully Sir Isaac and the other mages present realized something was very wrong right away. They overpowered Alcase before he could finish the activation spell, thanks the gods. After examining the Universum, Newton and the other mages concluded that fully activating the device would have almost certainly destroyed Earth ... and everything else within a billion miles or so."

"Wow. Sir Isaac Newton saved the day," Larry murmured, wonder in his words.

"Yep. Brilliant man," Midnight agreed, eyes brightening with the memory. "And wise with it, unlike that rat bastard, Alcase."

"You knew Sir Isaac Newton?" Larry eyed Midnight with growing respect. "Wait, exactly how old are you, cat? Don't tell me you were Newton's Familiar?"

"Nope," Midnight replied with a heavy sigh. "Unfortunately, I was that moron Alcase's Familiar. I warned him many times about the dangers of creating the Universum, but did he listen? No!" Midnight gave Larry a narrow-eyed glare. "And, in answer to your impertinent query about my age. It's none of your doggie business."

Still fascinated, despite Midnight's rebuke, Larry asked, "So what happened next? How did Newton and the other mages convince Alcase not to try again with the Universum?"

Silence descended as Larry and Carb waited breathlessly for Midnight to explain. "Well?" They chorused.

Midnight smiled, cold satisfaction filling her eyes. "Newton and the other mages reported Alcase to the Supernatural Council. They tried him and found him guilty of the grave misuse of magical power." The smile slipped from her feline face. "Alcase died while in prison, awaiting his execution. After that, the Council brought together the wisest and most powerful mage scientists of the time to study the Universum so they could figure out how to destroy the damned thing without activating it and obliterating the galaxy. They failed."

Larry eyed the cat skeptically. "Well, since the cosmos is still standing ... mostly, I'm assuming you mean they failed at destroying the Universum but succeeded at not activating it."

"Correct, you brilliant canine." Midnight congratulated Larry as if he were a particularly dense student who had surprised his teacher with an unexpectedly astute observation. "The Supernatural Council advisors realized that any attempt to destroy the Universum would automatically activate its power, thus destroying the earth, the stars, and everything beyond."

The cat heaved a dejected sigh. Her ears flattened and her shoulders drooped, as if she carried the weight of the world on her back. Midnight's next words confirmed that was indeed the case. "Since Alcase was the one to bring the Universum into being, the Supernatural Council decreed his descendants would be responsible for hiding and protecting the magical abomination. The Council tasked his family with keeping the Universum safe and hiding it well, down through the generations, so that no magical being can ever get their grubby little power-hungry hands on the damn thing."

Her chest puffing with pride, Midnight added, "There was some good news for me, though. At the request of Newton and the Supernatural Council, DEAF assigned me as the Felinus Universum. My job was, and still is, to assist each mage in the family line to keep the Universum safe and out of the wrong hands." Her whiskers curved up in a feline grin. "I guess they figured a cat, with its supreme disregard for the opinions of mages—and everyone else, would be a good counterpoint in case any of Alcase's descendants developed power hungry ideas about activating the Universum."

Larry nodded in understanding and couldn't help giving Midnight an amused grin. "Felinus Universum, huh? That's F.U. Boy, the boffins at DEAF really do love their acronyms, don't they?" He snickered. "And they have no freaking idea how stupid most of them sound."

Midnight licked her paw, then wiped it over her ear and down her face, but Larry spotted her reluctant smile, despite the attempted distraction.

CARB BROUGHT the group back to the present situation with a bump. "So, the deal is that Ted is currently the mage in charge of the Universum, right? And he's been kidnapped and is being tortured to get him to lower the scrapyard's wards. Then we have the baddies from the Council, who are also trying to gain access through wards, using Jesse and Larry as their stooges. Either way, it seems the bad guys are a hair's breadth away from getting their hands on the Universum and raining destruction on all of us. Does that about sum things up? So, what do we do now?"

Silence reigned as the trio eyed each other in growing dismay.

After several tense moments, the three reluctant heroes sighed in unison, already knowing what had to be done.

"Time to save the galaxy," Midnight meowed.

"We're gonna need some help," Larry replied.

"Agreed," Carb added with a soft belch. Those screws really could repeat on him.

11

NOBODY LISTENS

Larry slept in the next morning, not waking until he heard the kibble hit his bowl. After a good stretch, he hopped out of bed and bounded into the kitchen. He had no intention of missing the most important meal of the day.

As he crunched through his breakfast, Larry eyed Jesse over the metal rim of his bowl. She'd magicked her hair a strange shade of purply silver. Permed-tightened curls swirled over her scalp, glinting in the morning light. A thick pair of plastic reading glasses hung from a beaded chain around her neck. The glasses rested on a magically enhanced bosom that was propped up with an industrial-strength bra and covered with a pale pink sweatshirt. To top off her senior disguise, she wore a pair of hot pink velour sweatpants that assaulted the eyes.

When Jesse turned her back to pour another cup of coffee, Larry squinted at her backside. Was that writing on the seat of her sweatpants? Yep. In pale pink embroidery, the word 'Juicy' covered both cheeks. "Holy crap, Jesse, could you have made yourself look any more like a senior stereotype?"

Jesse turned from the coffeepot, grinning wickedly. "At least I left out the walker."

Larry mutely shook his head and turned his attention back to his bowl. Even Jesse's outrageous getup wasn't enough to put him off his food. His name wasn't Larry the Kibble Guy for nothing.

AFTER BREAKFAST, Larry tried to discuss the significant results of his first night patrol with Jesse. The third time he had to bark for her attention, he gave up. He'd told her about meeting Carb and about the strange goings on at the scrapyard prior to their arrival. He had even mentioned Midnight's return and Ted's kidnapping, but Jesse was too busy choosing just the right old lady purse to listen.

"Do you think a purple purse is too much? It clashes with my hair, doesn't it?" Jesse magicked the violent purple purse away and a salmon pink one appeared in its place. "How about this one?"

"Alright. I give up. You go have fun at the senior center, old lady," Larry told her with a frustrated growl. "I'll continue working on things here and see what I can do about organizing the office." The office's filthy state had horrified Larry the previous evening when he had helped Midnight create a nest for her kittens in the messy room. "Maybe I can get our Brownie to help me clean the place," he muttered.

A faint voice floated into the kitchen. "Nope. No help. House is my domain. You're on your own with the mess in the office."

Larry sighed gustily. He wouldn't get any help whipping the scrapyard into shape, would he? And no one wanted to hear about the many dangers lurking just outside the rusty scrapyard fence ... or about the potentially galaxy-destroying Universum hidden within.

He tried to fight a feeling of déjà vu. For months before the 'coven catastrophe', Larry had suspected something was amiss within the coven and that Mabel needed his help to deal with it successfully. However, despite his many offers, Mabel had stubbornly refused to share her concerns. Instead of making her listen, or investigating himself, he had allowed her assurances that she had things under control to placate him into inaction. Now Mabel was dead, and her coven was under enemy management—and it was all his fault.

Larry shook himself from nose to tail. No point going down that rabbit hole of guilt. The only thing he could do now was to make sure it didn't happen again. He vowed to work with Carb and Midnight to protect the Universum and help them come up with a plan to rescue Ted. Then he'd make Jesse sit down and listen to him so they could face the danger together. And save the galaxy.

Why did no one listen anymore? Larry felt every one of his four-plus centuries. The more things changed, the more they stayed the same. No one ever listened. Not even to themselves.

It was time to listen to his instincts—and well past time to take decisive action to fix things. He would not lose another magical partner, of fail at protecting those around him, no matter what it took.

AFTER JESSE LEFT in search of the senior center, Larry got to work. First, he lavishly praised the house Brownie's immaculate housekeeping, laying on one compliment after another until the saccharine sweetness of his praise made him slightly nauseous.

Finally, the little Brownie peeked out from behind the

pantry door, her mud-brown felt hat askew. "What do you want? I know what you're trying to do. The answer is 'no'. I'm not helping you clean the office, fur-face."

"Not even for a quart of magical nectar?" Larry eyed the Brownie, brows raised in polite query.

"Not even for ... what?" The Brownie's gaze narrowed, hope and skepticism warring for prominence in her chocolate brown eyes. "And where exactly are you going to get a quart of magical nectar?"

Larry grinned. He knew he had her now. "I have feathered friends in high places. They'll be visiting regularly, and have promised to bring me anything I need, if I ask nicely." He hoped he was right. Sid had promised to visit once they settled in. Surely, he could bribe Sid to bring a jar of nectar from the coven's storeroom on his trip.

Sighing deeply, he realized that his twin investigations would mean accruing more than a few debts of honor. He'd have to start a list of bribes, so he didn't lose track of what he owed and to whom.

"You promise, Familiar? I know you can't break your word if you promise. A quart of magical nectar in exchange for cleaning up that pigsty of an office. Agreed?" The Brownie grabbed a broom and narrowed her eyes at Larry.

"Agreed. I promise," Larry replied, nodding solemnly.

SEVERAL HOURS LATER, Larry gazed around the now spotless office in amazement. He knew Brownies were good at cleaning, but damn. The place didn't even look like the same office.

"Don't forget your promise, Familiar. You owe me a quart of magical nectar. My name is Violet - just so you know who will track you down if you don't keep your word." The little Brownie wiped her sweaty face and frowned ferociously at Larry. "I guarantee the office hasn't looked this good in half a century." She tucked several strands of thick, blond hair back under her cap and smiled fondly at the kittens mewing in their newly cleaned nursery under the desk.

"A promise is a promise." Larry held in a smile and nodded in agreement. "You'll get your nectar, Miss Violet, but it may be a moon or two. I'll have my raven friend bring it on his first visit."

Larry surveyed the spic and span office, which now looked like it would be a pleasant place to work. Not that Jesse had any intention of working, he reflected wryly.

He gave the hardworking Brownie a last dollop of praise. "Your hard work is most appreciated, Violet. Your skills as a Brownie are second to none."

"Oh, knock it off, Familiar. No need to keep up the brown-nosing. You got what you wanted, and soon I'll get my reward." Violet's brow lowered in warning and she snarled, "And I better get it."

"Never fear ma'am. I never break my word, once given. You'll get your nectar." Larry gave Violet a doggie grin, while he inwardly committed to ensure the Brownie got her nectar, no matter what.

He really didn't want to know what the little Fae would do if he didn't keep his word, but he knew it would be bad. Like hiding his kibble for a month. Or worse ... hiding the takeaway menus for good.

12

THE LADIES IN BLACK ... AND PURPLE

After the Brownie left, Larry searched the office. He'd hoped to find some information about the location of the powerful magical machine he knew lay buried somewhere beneath the scrapyard's moldering mounds of metal. However, there were no records or other evidence in the office to suggest a location for the Universum. In fact, there wasn't much of anything useful in the way of paperwork at all.

Larry snorted. The previous manager may have been a whizz at creating magical wards, but he was crap at mundane record-keeping. Hmmmm. He cocked his head, considering. Maybe that was on purpose. After all, Ted knew the Universum was extremely magical and very dangerous. Perhaps hiding it in a poorly run scrapyard was a genius move. Absolutely no one would think to look for the darn thing in the almost-forgotten magical backwater that was O'Malley's Supernatural Scrapyard.

Worry tensed Larry's shoulders, and his stomach rumbled with concern. Or hunger. More likely both, he philosophized. He headed back to the house in search of some lunch. He always thought better on a full stomach.

As Larry finished his midday kibble, Jesse's key jiggled in the front door lock. He had heard several voices besides Jesse's whispering and giggling long before their arrival at the front door, so he knew Jesse had brought company home. First things first, though. He swallowed the last piece of kibble and licked the bowl clean.

"Larry? Larry! Are you in here? I brought some new friends home for lunch." A wheedling tone entered Jesse's voice. "I even brought enough food for you."

Larry smothered a grin, wondering idly why Jesse was feeling guilty enough that she felt the need to bribe him with people food. Not that he'd turn it down. Oh, no. His momma didn't raise no dummy. Eat first and ask questions later.

Wearing her uncomfortable orthopedic shoes, Jesse hobbled into the kitchen, followed by a gaggle of senior ladies sporting hair in various shades of purple, pink, and blue. They all wore velour sweatpants or loose, flowery dresses, and each sported their own version of the chunkiest and ugliest costume jewelry Larry had ever seen.

Larry fought hard not to snicker. Or cower. Soon, all the old ladies had crowded around him, oohing and aaahing over his handsome good looks. *Couldn't fault them there,* he mused. Larry knew he was the most handsome magical junkyard dog ever.

With his muscular body, jet-black fur touched with brown on his muzzle, and huge blocky head reflecting his bully breed heritage, what wasn't there to like?

He knew he had been very lucky during his last trip to the Department of Eternal Animal Familiars after his previous incarnation. Mort, his assigned case worker at DEAF—and the most miserable demon alive, in Larry's opinion, had thankfully been on vacation when Larry arrived. The nice female temp filling in for that waste of space had responded to Larry's flattery and assigned him the massive Rottie-Pitt mix Familiar body of his dreams.

Larry wanted to keep his impressive canine form as long as possible. However, knowing Mort, and admitting his own tendency to piss off his perpetually miserable case worker, Larry feared his next physical body would probably be that of a toad. Or worse, a cat. He shivered in remembered revulsion. His cat incarnations ... all two of them, had left him mentally scarred for eternity. Eeew. If he never drank a warm bowl of milk again, it would be too soon.

A tantalizing scent tickled Larry's nose, pulling him out of his dour musings. "Is that meatloaf I smell? And mashed potatoes?" Larry groaned in anticipation. "Baclava for dessert? You've found a Greek diner, haven't you, Jesse?" Yum.

THE TALLEST OF the old ladies took a special liking to Larry, fixing him his very own plate of delicious diner food. If Jesse hadn't put a stop to it, she might have pulled up a chair for him, too.

"Cerri, no," Jesse scolded her new friend. "Larry's a ... dog. He can eat on the floor."

Feeling the brunt of Larry's irritated side-eye, Jesse added, "Besides, there's barely enough room for all of us ladies at the table."

Cerri gave Larry a warm smile, her eyes twinkling with suppressed mirth. "Well, at least let's put his plate next to my chair. That way, he'll still feel like he's part of our gathering."

As the ladies at the table chattered over their meal, Larry slowly savored his portion on the floor next to Cerri's chair. During the meal, she slipped several more juicy tidbits from the table onto his plate, earning his undying canine gratitude.

Out of ingrained habit Larry mind-spoke a thank you to his new best friend.

"You're welcome, Familiar."

Cerri's mind-spoken reply almost caused Larry to choke on his next mouthful. Not that he was all that surprised at her magical mind speaking ability. Instinctively, he'd known that she—and the rest of the supposed old ladies gathered around the table, were actually powerful witches the moment they had arrived.

"So, you lot are witches then, Cerri." Larry tilted his head and mind-spoke his question at the older woman currently peering down at him.

"Stating the obvious, Familiar?" Cerri's knowing eyes crinkled in mirth as she silently replied.

"And, judging by your old lady getups, I'm assuming you're all in disguise for some reason."

Cerri reached down and patted Larry's head, then scratched the perfect spot behind his left ear, making his leg twitch in pleasure.

Resolutely remembering his vow, Larry overcame an urge to give in to Cerri's ministrations and just enjoy the moment. He straightened up and asked, *"Why are such powerful witches all magicked up to resemble a gaggle of extremely senior AARP members?"*

"Nothing wrong with being an AARP member, Larry. It gets you great senior discounts at lots of places," Cerri replied with a sly grin.

"Now you're just teasing me," Larry protested. He sprawled on the cool tiles of the kitchen floor, just out of Cerri's reach. *"Seriously, why the disguises? I know most of you aren't past middle age, in witch years. And why are you all hanging out at the Catholic Church's senior center, anyway, since I'm assuming that's where you met Jesse? When she left here this morning, she told me she was going to a Bingo game there."*

"We're semi-retired, Larry. Mostly." Cerri grinned. *"And the*

Senior Center down the road provides excellent cover for our, uh, activities. Plus, who doesn't love a good game of church Bingo? And the cash prizes rock!"

She coaxed Larry back to her side with a piece of Baclava, then gave him a last pat on the head before addressing the chattering women out loud. "Ladies, I think it's time to talk strategy. Can we please all quiet down?"

The gathered witches immediately ceased their conversations and turned as one to face Cerri. Or rather, their leader, Larry realized with a start.

Cerri directed a nod of acknowledgement at Jesse. "If you don't mind, Jesse, I'll chair today's meeting."

"I don't mind at all. While I'm glad you're all here, I must admit it shocked me to run into you at the senior center today." Jesse's words were welcoming, but her gaze remained wary. "I wasn't aware the supposed goings on at the scrapyard merited the attention of the Supernatural Council."

At a glance from Cerri, a diminutive witch with light blue hair that clashed horribly with her orange velour track suit rose to her feet and addressed Jesse. "Hello ma'am. I'm Risa, Cerri's second-in-command. Thank you for hosting today's meeting. Cerri has asked me to bring you and Larry up to speed on our investigation."

Jesse's lips curved in an agreeable smile, but her face reflected doubt. "I'm still not sure why the Supernatural Council has called in the elite members of the Brew Crew to investigate the disappearance of the manager of a nearly derelict magical scrapyard. Surely, the man just got bored with the job and took off for parts unknown? Besides, Larry and I are here now. We can keep an eye on things from now on."

An uncomfortable silence descended on the gathering.

Frowning, Cerri broke the tense pause. "Jesse, I'd appreciate it if you didn't refer to my team as the 'Brew Crew.' I know there are those in the supernatural community who don't respect or appreciate the work we do, but until now, I didn't count you among them. As you know, those seated around this table are all powerful and experienced potion witches. My elite team handles sensitive matters for the Supernatural Bureau of Investigation. We're here at the request of the Supernatural Council."

Larry snorted in surprise. "Holy shit! You guys are undercover SBI agents!" He scurried over to Jesse's chair and barked. "See? I told you something hinky's going on here. I just knew it!"

Jesse's truculent frown told Larry his magical partner still wasn't completely convinced.

"Larry is right, Jesse." Cerri's voice reflected the gravity of her words. "There's a lot more going on here than you know. The SBI dispatched my team to the area several weeks ago, just after the previous manager's disappearance." She gestured at her second-in-command and said, "Please, let's all listen to Risa's recap."

Risa resumed her report and spoke of magical mobsters, kidnapping, and corruption in high places. She even briefly mentioned the Universum, but didn't go into detail about what it could do.

Larry listened intently, nodding occasionally as Risa confirmed things he already knew and explained other things he hadn't. Dammit. He had known something wasn't right at the scrapyard as soon as they arrived, but he never dreamed he and Jesse had walked unwittingly into a dangerous hunt for a device that could destroy the galaxy.

During Risa's report, Jesse's fingers tapped a staccato rhythm on her knee. When Risa had finished, Jesse jumped up and started clearing the table. "Would you look at this mess? I'm glad everyone enjoyed the food. Thanks for the Greek diner recommendation, Cerri. I'm gonna clean up now."

13

CERRIDWEN'S PRIESTESS

Jesse bustled between the kitchen and the table, and several other witches rose to help her.

While Jesse and the others were busy with the cleanup, Cerri sighed and met Larry's worried gaze. She lowered her voice but spoke aloud. "Your magical partner either doesn't understand the danger or doesn't want to ... or, well, let's talk about that later. I need your help to solve this, Larry. I'm not overstating things when I say that the fate of the galaxy may just rest with you and Jesse."

"Well, Fuck. So much for Jesse's plans for semi-retirement and my wish for a quiet life," Larry snorted.

"My sentiments, exactly, Familiar," Cerri replied as she rose from the table and gestured toward the front door. "How about you and I take a walk and discuss things, Larry?"

"Can I have one more piece of that delicious dessert before we go?"

With an amused chuckle, Cerri gave Larry a small piece of the remaining baclava. "That's it, bud. This stuff is so sweet it'll rot your teeth out. Then how would you eat your kibble?"

"Oh, I'd find a way." Larry snickered.

"I don't doubt it, you chowhound. Shall we?" Cerri led the way outside into the late afternoon sunlight and the duo ambled toward the hulking metal mountains in amiable silence.

As they walked, the sun darkened, and gray clouds crowded in as the sun sank lower in the sky. Their lunch meeting had run very late; afternoon was quickly slipping into evening. Larry shivered in the unexpected chill, then glanced over at his walking companion. "So, you're a supervising agent with the SBI, Cerri?"

"Yep. Part time these days, though. As I mentioned earlier, I'm semi-retired."

Larry snorted and gave her a disbelieving side-eye. "Yeah, right. I don't buy that any more than I buy your old lady act. Also, why did Jesse refer to your team as the Brew Crew?" Larry knew he'd likely touch a nerve by mentioning Jesse's derisive words about Cerri's team, but he couldn't help himself.

Cerri grimaced and kicked a piece of rusty metal back toward the heap it had fallen from. "My team is comprised of Water and Earth witches, Larry, which means our magical powers involve making and using magical potions or spells. Hence Jesse's derogatory use of the term 'Brew Crew.'"

A bitter smile twisted the SBI agent's lips. "As you know, Jesse is a Fire witch. Fire and Air witches consider themselves superior to the rest of us, as they can control their elements directly, while most Water and Earth witches must brew or otherwise create our magic indirectly by using objects or potions made of the base element we control."

"Oh, now I get it, I guess. But I'm sure Jesse didn't mean her comment as an insult," Larry said, stoutly defending his new partner, even though she had been rude.

"Perhaps not. But Jesse is a Fire Witch, so forgive me if I remain in doubt," Cerri replied dryly.

When she drew to a stop, Larry realized they had walked the length of the scrapyard. A tall chain-link fence topped with razor-wire blocked their path. "Guess it's time to head back," he muttered.

"Not yet, Familiar. You and I need to finish our chat." Cerri paused next to a mature oak tree and knelt, placing her hands flat on the bare earth. She inhaled deeply, then lowered her head as if in meditation. After a moment she nodded once, seemingly satisfied, then sat crossed legged under the tree.

She smiled and patted a spot next to her. "Come, sit, Larry. We are well out of range of all eyes and ears."

Intrigued, Larry ambled over and sat next to Cerri. "So, you're an Earth witch?" He asked, then it hit him. "Wait a minute. Cerri ... Cerridwen. Holy shit! You're a Priestess of Cerridwen, the Celtic creator goddess, aren't you? The Supernatural Council sure has sent in the big guns."

He rolled his eyes and whined, "This damned scrapyard is smack dab in the middle of a super dangerous hot mess, isn't it? One bad enough that the Celtic creator goddess has taken notice. Well, shit. It's just my luck."

Cerri's smile had turned into a full-blown grin while Larry ranted. "Yes, Familiar, I'm an Earth witch. And yes, Cerridwen is my patron goddess, and she has an ... interest in what is happening here." The priestess and part-time SBI agent laughed, the deep rich sound ringing in the air. "And I guess you could say the SBI has sent in the 'big guns.' My team handles sensitive cases that call for discretion—and a whole lot of magical power, which I assure you, my team has in spades."

Larry decided he'd better up his respect level. "I don't doubt it, ma'am. How can Jesse and I help?"

"First, drop the ma'am. Cerri is just fine. Second, I need your agreement that what I'm about to tell you remains confidential ... even from Jesse." Cerri's serious gaze backed up her request for confidentiality.

"Even from Jesse?" Larry frowned. "Now wait just a minute. I can't keep secrets from my magical partner! That's how I ... we wound up in this goddess-forsaken magical scrapyard in the back of beyond. Our former High Priestess kept dangerous secrets from Jesse and me, and we were too self-involved to press her for answers, so we could help."

Larry's ears drooped. "And now Mabel's dead. And here we are."

CERRI GENTLY STROKED Larry's head. "Larry, as you have just stated, we have a major magical situation with world-ending repercussions on our hands. There is a lot you don't know, most of which I'll share with you now. The thing is, though, while I might think Jesse is one of the 'good guys', I must confirm that before I can fully bring her into the operation. Of course, she must know there is an investigation. That's unavoidable. But she cannot know the whole of it yet."

She lifted Larry's muzzle gently so she could meet his eyes with her keen gaze. "Do you understand, Familiar?"

Larry pulled his head out of Cerri's grip and took a step back, frowning in confusion. "But why do you trust me and not Jesse? We both came from the same coven."

His eyes widened when illumination struck. "Crap! Litha really does have her grubby fingers in this, doesn't she? Her co-conspirator on the Council is the one who talked the Witch Council into sending Jesse and me here. So, I'll ask again. Why do you trust me, but not Jesse?"

"Your loyalty to your new magical partner is admirable, Familiar," Cerri told him. "Regarding how I know I can trust you ... I can read your heart, my dear. Familiars are creatures of the earth, are they not? Created by and powered through Earth magic? You have no deception in you, Larry." Cerri's wise gaze didn't waver. "However, Jesse is a Fire witch, as is Litha ...."

"Jesse has about as much in common with Litha as I do with that toadstool over there," Larry spat. He angrily jerked his head toward a cluster of pale green mushrooms attached to a rotting branch resting against the perimeter fence. "She wouldn't throw water on Litha if she were on fire."

Reconsidering, he added, "In fact, Jesse would more likely be the one to light that bitch on fire. Being a Fire witch, that'd be right up her alley." He shook himself all over, snorting in disgust at Cerri's vile insinuations.

Cerri chuckled and dipped her head in mute agreement, and the tense atmosphere lightened a bit. "I have a deal for you, Larry. How about you and I discuss what's happened so far and where we think the investigation needs to go from here? Then we can talk further about how ... or if Jesse can fit into the picture?"

Larry realized that Cerri's offer was the best he was likely to get. "Deal," he replied, then he recalled his late-night conversation with Carb and Midnight. "Oh, and I might have a few tidbits of information you'll find useful as well. I'm, uh, assuming, since you already know about the Universum, that me telling you what I know about it won't end with my death ...."

"Took a life oath not to talk about it, did you? Who bound you to that, I wonder?" Cerri's mouth curved in an understanding grin. "As long as whoever bound you to the life oath was careful with their wording, you should be fine."

While Larry considered Cerri's words, Midnight slunk into the tree's dappled light and came to a stop a few feet away.

The feline Familiar bowed her head slightly and raised one paw in deference. "Hail and Welcome, Priestess of Cerridwen. My name is Midnight and I'm the ... uh, Familiar to Ted. He's the mage who is—was in charge of this scrapyard. Larry and I will share what information we can with you, ma'am."

Midnight grinned at Larry and added, "And I was very careful in my wording of the life oath kibble-breath; no harm will come to you while we resolve this matter, as long as your heart is pure, and your intentions are good."

Cerri smiled down at the small black cat. "Thank you for joining us, Midnight. As the Felinus Universum and Familiar to the Universum's current Guardian, I'm sure you have much to share. Oh, and congratulations on your litter of feline Familiars. I'm glad you have now brought them to safety, and I applaud your extensive efforts on behalf of your magical partner." She chuckled at the shocked expression on Midnight's face.

Midnight quickly covered her surprise and accepted Cerri's congratulations. "Uh, thank you, ma'am. So, you know who ... what I am, then. You know about the Universum and about the current crowd of bad guys after it." She nodded once and added, "Let's get started."

Larry, Cerri, and Midnight talked and strategized well into the evening. After the moon rose above the trees, they sat in silence, faces tilted toward the night sky as they gazed at the stars twinkling above.

"Hello, demon." Cerri didn't take her eyes off the sky, but her focus shifted to a messy pile of rusted metal near the fence. "Why don't you come out from there and introduce yourself?"

After a moment, the metal mound shifted, and Carb's squat, green figure scrambled out. He bowed deeply at Cerri and gave a short but formal speech. "Hail and welcome, Priestess of Cerridwen. I am Carb, the ferrous demon in charge of this scrapyard. If I can be of service, please don't hesitate to ask."

Cerri's lips twitched, but she smothered her smile. "Hello, Carb. Please, call me Cerri. On behalf of the Supernatural Council, I thank you for taking such good care of the scrapyard and the powerful magic it holds."

Carb bowed again, his enormous nose almost hitting the ground as he did. "You are most welcome, Cerri." His face wrinkled with worry as he rose from his bow. "But I'm afraid your praise might be misplaced, ma'am. I've been doing the best I can without leaving the scrapyard, but the bad guys kidnapped Ted, anyway. And Midnight went after him and had her kittens in an alley far from home. If only I'd been brave enough to leave the scrapyard to tell someone about what happened."

The little demon shook his head. "I mean, I told that Witch Council guy when he showed up, but then nothing happened …."

"How about we move past the recriminations and talk about what we can do next, Carb?" Cerri patted the ground. "Come, sit. Larry and Midnight have filled me in on what's happened so far." She smiled at the little demon slyly. "However, since I know you've been behind that pile of metal for most of the time we chatted, you already know that. Did they miss anything? Or do you have anything else to tell us that might help?"

Carb plopped to the ground next to Cerri, his face scrunched in thought. "Um, maybe I should mention the half dozen magically shielded mages scoping out the scrapyard right now? They've been here almost every night, but they haven't been able to get past the wards. Yet."

Larry started and gazed around anxiously. The mages must be extremely powerful if they could shield themselves so well that he couldn't sense them. He glanced over at Cerri, whose calm expression told Larry that news of the mages lurking outside the fence line did not surprise her.

"You knew they're out there, Cerri," he growled.

"Yes, Familiar, I'm aware of their presence this evening. My team has been watching them for the past several weeks. While the mages outside the scrapyard are well-shielded, their feet must still touch the earth, or something resting upon it. Earth is my Element, as you know, so it's easy for me to sense them."

She sighed. "Too bad I'm not an Air witch, though. While I can sense their presence and location, I cannot hear their whispered words this evening. I have, however, been able to shield our presence ... and our words, from them."

CERRI SHIFTED her position and gestured the trio closer, her expression all business. "So, here's the recap, gentlemen—and lady. My SBI team knows Ted is the Guardian of the Universum, which is a powerful dark magic machine that can destroy the cosmos if it falls into the wrong hands. We also know he finagled an assignment to this scrapyard several decades ago so he could hide the Universum here amongst the more ordinary, broken pieces of magical machinery, no doubt hoping the general magical buzz of the supernatural scrapyard and its wards would help disguise the Universum's power."

After a pause, Cerri glanced apologetically at Midnight before adding, "Recently, word of the Universum and its location has reached those with nefarious intent. Either Ted hasn't been careful enough with his words and actions, or, as we suspect, there is a traitor in the Witches Council, or both. Only a few senior members of the Witch Council, besides Ted and certain trusted members of the Supernatural Council, know the tool is hidden here. Someone has been talking out of turn."

"Sounds like you're assuming the Supernatural Council isn't the source of the leak, right?" Larry asked his question in a neutral tone, not wanting to piss off the powerful priestess witch at his side. She worked for the Supernatural Bureau of

Investigation, which reported directly to the Supernatural Council, so her loyalties might prevent her from seeking corruption within her own organizational orbit.

"I'm positive the leak is not within the Supernatural Council or the SBI, Familiar." Cerri's words were clipped, her tone final.

Oops, definitely pissed her off, Larry reflected with chagrin. He met Cerri's gaze in mute apology.

Cerri chuckled and tugged gently on Larry's velvety ear. "Don't apologize for asking a legitimate question, Larry. I've worked for the SBI for almost a century. I trust my team and those within the SBI who have direct knowledge of this investigation. I also know that the Supernatural Council is as susceptible to corruption as any powerful organization. However, in this case I've already investigated and cleared those on the Council with direct knowledge of this matter—and that number is small, as information this sensitive is compartmented."

She gave Midnight and Larry a sympathetic look. "I'm afraid the leak is much closer to home. It is much more likely that Ted inadvertently revealed something or perhaps one of the rank-and-file members of Witch Council members recently discovered the secret."

INTO THE TENSE silence following Cerri's statement, Carb interjected. "Okay, so, sounds like we're all up to speed. But what do we do now?"

"Now, demon, we find the Universum, figure out how to spirit it away from here to a safe place, and then we neutralize the bad guys. We must succeed, or .... well, if we don't, it won't matter anymore. To anyone. In any realm. Anywhere." Cerri rubbed her hands over her face with a heavy sigh.

Larry's ears perked, head swiveling to meet Cerri's knowing gaze. "You mean the damn thing will destroy all the supernatural realms, not just the earth and the surrounding galaxy?"

Cerri's warning was stark. "We suspect that, if the Universum is activated, it will destroy both the galaxy and many of the supernatural realms—no matter where they are physically located. Any realm that has a portal or Crossroads link to Earth or anywhere else within this galaxy will also suffer catastrophic destruction."

Midnight's chest rumbled with an angry growl and Larry whined in distress.

Carb's normally upright ears sleeked back against his head. "*All* the other realms? The Underworld, Faery, Mount Olympus, Naraka, Asgard ... and the rest, all gone?" The angry demon's mouth curled in a snarl. "Why would anyone create such a devastating magical machine? And how the hell did they plan to survive its use?"

"Why did Alcase create it?" Midnight asked rhetorically. "Because he could." Her muzzle crinkled in disgust, revealing razor sharp feline fangs. "Mages do not differ from humans in that respect. In the pursuit of knowledge and power, they often pay scant attention to the devastating damage their inventions can cause—even to themselves."

She sighed in frustration and continued. "We should probably skip the centuries-old recriminations for now. We have more immediate problems. One reason I stayed away from the scrapyard so long is that, as long as I stayed near the old marina, Ted could communicate with me from his holding cell on a fancy-ass ship moored nearby. I couldn't get too close, so I didn't hear his captor's plans, but ... Ted's pain and thoughts, when questioned, told me enough."

Midnight sneezed delicately and summed up. "Bottom line: it seems there's a powerful criminal mage who wants the Universum and he'll stop at nothing to get it. I'm fuzzy on what he plans to do with it or if he knows that it's impossible to use the device without destroying everything and everyone ... including himself."

Cerri nodded at Midnight, her gaze serious. "Our investigations have revealed that much. However, we have yet to discover the mage's purpose in seeking the Universum. It is good that you know where his henchmen are keeping Ted. We must free him before he—"

"Ted will never reveal the location of the Universum. He'll die first." Midnight's plaintive meow sliced through the air. "And that time is coming fast. He can't hold out much longer-rrrr—." Her last words ended with a grief-stricken yowl.

After a moment of grief-filled silence, the little cat firmly shook off her distress. "Yes, I know exactly where the bad guys are keeping Ted. That's one reason I came back to the scrapyard. Yesterday, Ted sensed that 'friendlies' had approached the scrapyard's wards."

Midnight glanced at Larry and added, "He could sense your and Jesse's good intentions and realized that you had been sent to replace him as manager of the scrapyard. He keyed the wards to allow you and Jesse entry, then he made me leave him on that stupid ship and travel back here with the kittens. He wanted me to warn you and to seek your help."

"And help you both shall have, Familiar." Cerri's words resonated with reassurance and resolve.

ARE WE WINNING YET?

"Number five, man alive. That's number five, man alive, ladies and gents." The Bingo caller's sonorous voice echoed through the senior center's massive main hall. Scores of elderly attendees, eyes down, assiduously filled in their multiple Bingo cards with thick, colored markers. Tension filled the air.

"BINGO!" A sharp voice cut through the haze of concentration, enlivening the masses, who turned their sharpened gazes on the supposed Bingo winner. "I checked, and it's definitely Bingo this time," the speaker muttered defensively. The massive multicolored pompom on the man's knit hat bounced crazily as he nodded enthusiastically.

A grizzled elder in a Yankees baseball hat shouted insults at the purported winner. "Yeah, like the last three times you thought you had Bingo ... and you didn't. They should'a banned you already, you old goat."

The Bingo caller attempted to dispel the air of suspicion around the pompom man's supposed win. "Okay, Tony, why don't you shout out your Bingo numbers, and we'll check to see if you have a winning card."

As Tony called out his numbers, Jesse, presently seated at a large table in the hall's corner with her new SBI friends, aired her grievance. "How come we can't play Bingo while we have our strategy meeting? I don't know about you lot, but I can mark Bingo cards and listen at the same time. And why the heck are we meeting here, anyway?"

Cerri eyed Jesse with determined patience. "As I explained when we chose this venue, Jesse, I'm afraid the scrapyard may now have unfriendly ears listening to our conversations. Midnight caught two large rats early this morning. She told me they are the first ones she's ever seen inside the scrapyard, as most non-magical creatures avoid the powerful energy surrounding the place. Unfortunately, one rat turned out to be a Familiar, heavily spelled to resemble a mundane rat, which is likely how he got past the scrapyard's wards. The Familiar refuses to identify his magical partner, but I suspect it's not someone on our side."

"Yeah, yeah. I get it," Jesse grumbled. "But why the Bingo Hall? It's like leading a horse to water but not letting them drink. I absolutely love Bingo."

Larry, who was huddled under the table and on his best canine behavior while pretending to be the Service Dog Jesse had claimed him to be, poked her with his nose and mind-spoke a soft rebuke.

"Jesse, you know this is a great place to meet. Cerri's illusion spell around our table makes it appear that you're all just a bunch of oldsters, busily marking your Bingo cards, more interested in winning the Bingo prize than saving the galaxy. What villain, magical or otherwise, would suspect a bunch of blue- and purple-haired senior citizens of conspiring to disrupt his evil machinations during a freaking Bingo game?"

Around the table, heads nodded, confirming that Larry had shared his mind-spoken words of wisdom with the group, and that everyone agreed with his reasoning.

"Whose side are you on, anyway? You're supposed to be my Familiar." Jesse replied aloud, giving Larry an evil grin. "Or, rather, my Service Dog."

Larry regarded his magical partner with stubborn, sad eyes. "I'm your Familiar alright, Jesse. And I'm not about to make the same mistake I made with Mabel when I ignored my gut, buried my head in the sand, and let her convince me she could handle the coven issues on her own ... and it got her killed. I'm gonna make you listen, Jesse, and you and I are gonna help these nice SBI agents arrest the bad guys and save the galaxy. Understood, old lady?"

Jesse bristled. "Who are you calling old, fur-ball? You've got at least a couple centuries on me!"

"Well, if you will dress in those ridiculous velour track suits with writing on the butt and magic your hair that awful shade of silvery blue—"

A sharp crack echoed off the transparent walls of the containment spell surrounding the table and its occupants as Cerri's hand smacked the table's wooden surface. "That's enough, you two! We've got a lot of work to do, so listen up, everyone." Cerri gave her second-in-command a firm nod and instructed her to give her report.

RISA ROSE from her seat next to Jesse, her diminutive size bringing her eyes merely to the same height as the tallest of the witches seated around the table. Today, she wore a loose dress dotted with improbably large daisies floating in a cerulean blue sky. Around her neck hung several rows of plastic beads in a garish shade of yellow that clashed with the daisies. Her light blue hair, at least, matched her dress.

She cleared her throat and loosened her hold on the stack of papers in her hands. "Hello everyone. I've got a lot to report today, so let's get to it." She handed Jesse the papers and said, "Can you please take one and pass them along?"

Jesse mumbled a response but dutifully peeled off a sheet before passing the rest to the witch seated next to her.

Fixing a stern eye on the group, Risa began. "I will go through each item on the agenda and summarize our current knowledge. Please hold your questions until the end."

She shook her head at one attendee when the woman pulled a pen out of her purse. "No written notes, please. And I'll be taking these papers back at the end of today's briefing. We can't take any chances with this information, so please pay attention and take mental notes only."

"First item—our interrogation of the rat Familiar caught by Midnight has filled in a lot of blanks for us. We have now confirmed the identity of the mage who is seeking the Universum. His name is Michael Malfisco. He is the grandson of Carlos Giotti, head of the Giotti crime family, which has bases here in Bridgeport and also in Brooklyn. For the past several years, Michael has competed with several other grandsons for the role of heir apparent to Carlos."

Gasps echoed around the table at Risa's words. Obviously, the assembled witches had heard of the Giotti crime family.

Risa paused at everyone's shocked reaction, then nodded her agreement. "Yes, the case involving the Giotti family presents unique dangers. The family's traditional mob mentality, combined with their mage bloodline, along with their many connections in the supernatural world, means we will have our hands full dealing with them. From now on, information about this investigation is on a 'need to know' basis only."

Larry's stomach sank. Even he had heard of the exploits of the Giotti crime family and knew they used threats, intimidation, and murder, along with large amounts of magic, to hold their position as one of the richest and most powerful magical crime families on the East Coast.

He dredged his memory for the Giotti family structure and asked, "Why are the grandsons competing for the heir apparent title? What about the old man's children? Why aren't any of them in line to take over from their father?"

Risa acknowledged Larry's question with a nod. "Carlos' wife gave him several daughters, but only one son. His son died in a magical explosion several years ago. Being a traditionalist, Carlos would never allow a woman to head the family, which left his three daughters' half dozen male children—Carlos' grandsons—to duke it out amongst themselves for the heir apparent role."

She grimaced and added, "Carlos is a big believer in the survival of the fittest. He's letting his grandsons kill each other off until only one remains standing. Michael Malfisco, the mage who kidnapped Ted, is the son of Carlos' oldest daughter. He's one of only two grandsons still in competition for the heir-apparent prize. Our research tells that the other grandson, Anthony Manucci, is heavily favored to win the heir position from his grandfather, however Michael isn't out of the game yet. In fact ...."

She hesitated, then glanced at Cerri, who gestured for her to continue. "Last night, we captured one of the mages that have been spying on the scrapyard." Eyes glittering with something dark, she added, "With a small amount of 'encouragement', I got him to tell me what he knows. Apparently, Michael has decided he is no longer interested in winning the contest to be his grandfather's heir. He has altogether grander plans."

The atmosphere around the table tightened, all eyes focused on the petite but powerful witch's words.

Jesse broke the tense silence. "Well, get on with it, Risa. Tell us what you think this Michael character has planned that would have much of an impact on the supernatural world. Since the Giotti family restricts most of its criminal activity to the human realm, despite their magic, why should we worry? What makes you think this guy plans to go all 'major magical destruction' on the supernatural community?"

Cerri fixed Jesse with a narrow-eyed stare. "Jesse, you are here today because Larry has pled your case. He assures me you are on our side, and not a traitor to your witch oath, which, as you know, obligates you to strive to preserve and protect Earth and all its inhabitants—including humans. Please don't make me doubt the wisdom of my decision."

Eyes wide in disbelief, Jesse jumped to her feet, fists clenched. "Now wait just a minute! I've never betrayed my witch oath, nor would I. Who's been saying otherwise?! Hang on ... is that why you and Larry slunk off after lunch yesterday? To discuss my potential treachery?"

She shook her head in vigorous denial. "I've got nothing to do with this whole mess. I didn't get myself sent to manage this goddess-forsaken supernatural scrapyard on purpose, you know."

Her shoulders drooped and hurt reflected in her eyes. "Is that what you all suspect? That I'm one of the bad guys? That I had a hand in the death of my oldest friend and coven leader and that I'm possibly in league with the magical mob?"

Jesse angrily swiped at the tears streaking her cheeks, then pounded her fist on the table, an angry echo of Cerri's earlier gesture. "Come on then, being the all-powerful Brew crew—witches you are, one of you must have a truth spell on you. Lemme have it. I'll take it here and now to prove my loyalty and get this traitor sh—er stuff out of the way."

Larry pressed his body against Jesse's legs, and mind-spoke a caution. *"Calm down, partner. At this rate, you're more likely to be given a tantrum spell than a truth one. You realize that, looking at this from the outside, Cerri and her team have every right to question the convenience of our sudden reassignment to the scrapyard.*"

Jesse's face softened as she gazed down at her Familiar. He was right, of course. "*You may have a point, fur-butt. But that doesn't make their suspicion of me any easier to swallow.*"

"*No one's asking you to swallow anything, Jesse.*" Larry cocked his head thoughtfully. "*But offering to swallow a truth brew would be a major point in your favor.*"

"As if I need a truth brew. You can see my heart, bud. You know I'm no traitor," Jesse whispered as she stroked Larry's head softly, her hand still shaking from her angry outburst.

Larry locked eyes with his magical partner and mind-spoke his reply. "*Yes, I can see your heart, Jesse—but Cerri can't. You're a very powerful witch; no witch alive can see your heart unless you voluntarily reveal it.*"

He leaned his head into Jesse's hand and fixed beseeching eyes on hers. "*Take the truth brew, Jesse. Please. I—we need you fully on board with this. We both know what happened the last time we buried our heads in the sand, ignored potential danger, and left others to sort things out. Someone died ... Mabel died. We've gotta step up, partner.*"

After a tense moment, Jesse nodded reluctant acceptance and gave Larry's head a last pat. She heaved a resigned sigh, then rose.

Back straight, her determined gaze met that of each witch present before settling on Cerri. "Well, witches? Do any of you have a truth brew on hand? If so, I'll take it now. Then you can ask all the intrusive questions you like so I can prove my innocence, and we can get on with the business of saving the damn galaxy from this moron ... I mean, magical mobster."

∾

CERRI STUDIED JESSE SEARCHINGLY. Whatever she saw must have convinced her that Jesse was serious, because she nodded and gestured to a witch at the far end of the table. The witch she indicated was thin and stooped; she had pure white hair and sharp blue eyes surrounded by a maze of deep wrinkles.

Jesse stared at the wizened witch, realizing with a shock that the woman wasn't using an aging spell. She was legitimately ancient. At a guess, the elderly witch had to be well over three, maybe even four centuries old. Stomach tightening with nerves, Jesse just knew that this crone had had plenty of time over the past several centuries to perfect her brewing magic. Any truth potion this incredibly experienced witch concocted was going to be a humdinger.

Shaking off her fears, she reminded herself that she had nothing to hide. "Well, ma'am? Do you have a brew for me?"

"The name is Mary, dear. And I always come prepared." The ancient witch giggled. "Isn't that the Boy Scout motto? Always be prepared. Not that I was ever a Boy Scout, mind you. There was no such organization until quite recently. Plus, I'm a girl—I mean, a woman." She gave another wheezing laugh, but it did nothing to disguise the woman's penetrating, intelligent eyes.

Larry snickered, nudged Jesse's leg, and said, "I guess, if you have as many moons as this lovely witch, any organization that's 'only' one-hundred-something years old would still be considered relatively new. Oh, and I'm pretty sure the Boy Scouts allow girls now, but they may have an upper age limit." He nodded at the senior witch and coughed politely. "Pretty sure, ma'am, that you exceed the age limit by, uh, a few centuries or so."

A wave of snorts and snickers came from the witches seated around the table. Even their leader, Cerri, fought a smile at Larry's insouciant comments.

Jesse realized Larry had shared his thoughts with the group

to break the tension and to reassure her she was making the right decision by taking the truth brew. She glanced down at her Familiar and mind-spoke her gratitude. "Thanks, fur-face. That actually helped."

She then addressed the crone witch directly. "Mary, I apologize for my smart-mouthed Familiar. He's got no class. I'll take that truth brew now if you please."

Mary nodded and rummaged in her huge handbag, while muttering softly to herself. Finally, she exclaimed in success. "Ah-ha! I knew it was in here. Can never find anything in this benighted bag."

She drew out a small blue glass bottle and placed it triumphantly on the table. Thick liquid within the bottle swirled sluggishly. At a casual gesture from the ancient witch, the bottle fell on its side, then rolled down the table, before stopping directly in front of Jesse. It spun in a lazy circle, then righted itself, seemingly of its own accord.

Jesse took a moment to study the bottle and silently admire the elderly brewmaster's magical expertise. Get on with it, woman, she scolded herself. Swallowing in anticipation of the brew's no doubt disgusting taste, she grabbed the bottle, thumbed off the cork stopper, and gulped the viscous brew down.

After a moment, her mouth curved in an involuntary grin. "Hey, that tasted pretty good! A whole hell of a lot better than I expected. Most brews taste like old socks—not that I know what old socks taste like. Honest."

Realizing she was rambling, Jesse shut her mouth with a snap, then ventured a polite query. "Umm, is the truth serum already working? It is ... right?"

Mary's eyes twinkled with delight. "No, Jesse, the brew takes a few minutes to activate. But thank you for the compliment about the truth brew's pleasant taste. As your Familiar so aptly pointed out, I'm ... ah, a little old. What kind of centuries-old

Water witch would I be if I couldn't concoct a pleasant-tasting brew?"

While Mary spoke, Jesse's stomach fizzed and gurgled, then a creeping numbness spread out from her middle until it filled her whole body. Lightheaded and slightly dizzy, she suppressed an urge to panic. Instead, she allowed her body to fold awkwardly into the chair at her back. "Okay ... pretty sure the truth brew is working now, folks. Ask away."

The truth finding didn't take long. Afterwards, Jesse couldn't clearly remember either the questions the witches asked—or her answers. She only knew she spoke from the heart ... not just because she had no choice, but because she realized she wanted this group of witches to believe in her honorable intentions.

CERRI ENDED the questioning with a final query. "Do you have any questions for us, Jesse? We have asked our fill, and you have answered honestly. We find your heart to be pure and of good intent. Thank you for your cooperation."

Larry snorted and blurted, "It's not like Jesse had any choice in the answering honestly part."

Jesse gave Larry a none-to-gentle nudge with her foot. "Shut up, knucklehead. You're the one who encouraged me to take the damned truth brew in the first place."

"Listen, you old bat—" Larry sputtered.

A wave of relieved laughter interrupted Larry's riposte.

Someone asked, "Do you two always argue like an old married couple?"

The tension dissipated and even Cerri joined in the merriment enough to allow a small smile to curve her lips.

Once the laughter died down, she addressed the group. "Alright, everyone. Now that's out of the way, there's no need to guard our words. We all share the same goals ... to defeat the bad guys and rescue Ted ... oh, and save the galaxy while we're at it." She gestured at her second-in-command. "Risa, please finish your report."

Risa nodded once and continued, "As I mentioned earlier, Michael isn't really interested in inheriting his grandfather's earthbound crime syndicate. Instead, it appears he wants to create his own magical mob that is, quite literally, out of this world. The captured mage told me that Michael has only been fighting the battle of the grandsons to divert attention from his true plans. He knows he can't take on his grandfather directly anytime soon. Carlos Giotti is too strong ... and he is ruthless enough to have Michael killed if he attempts a coup. The mage was a little unclear on the next bit, but somehow, Michael found out about the astro-magical Universum buried and all but forgotten in the supernatural scrapyard, practically on his doorstep."

When Risa paused, the witches around the table leaned forward, eyes wide in anticipation of her next words.

"Out with it, Risa." Cerri encouraged her lieutenant to finish her report.

"Yes ma'am. The captured mage was perfectly clear on the next bit. Michael wants to steal the Universum and activate it. He plans to take his hand-picked henchmen and export his new criminal enterprise to the stars, leaving Earth, indeed this whole galaxy, in the dust. Quite literally."

Silence reigned for a moment, then pandemonium broke out, with the witches all talking over each other in confusion and horror.

"QUIET!" Cerri's voice rang with power.

Once silence blanketed the table, Cerri spoke in a more moderated tone, her gaze intent on Risa. "Did the mage explain exactly how Michael plans to get over the rather large activation hurdle? If the Universum is fully activated, its dark magic will destroy the earth ... and almost certainly the entire galaxy, in a matter of seconds. There simply isn't time to use the Universum to travel outside the galaxy before it destroys everything—including the person who activates it."

Risa shrugged; her mouth curved in a self-deprecating smile. "The mage couldn't tell me that, but I'm sure he would have if he knew. He did mention that he'd heard rumors of a powerful supernatural, in league with Michael, who knows of a way to delay the Universum's wave of destruction for several crucial seconds ... just enough time to use the machine to transport Michael and his henchmen to wherever in the mega-verse their black heart desires."

"BINGO!" A familiar voice penetrated the illusion spell surrounding the table and its occupants. Apparently, Tony the pompom man thought he had a winning hand. Again.

Larry, Jesse, and Cerri's team of SBI agents eyed each other with determination. They would have to take quick and decisive action to ensure the magical mobster and his co-conspirators didn't have the winning hand in this terrifying supernatural game, or all would be lost.

THE DEMONS DESCEND

Silvery shafts of moonlight highlighted the immense mountains of metal when the ferrous demons arrived. The Underworld creatures skittered and chittered, their squat green bodies impossibly agile as they scampered over the massive mounds, shoving bits of metal into their mouths as they went.

"Alright, guys, listen up! Pay attention!" Carb's commanding shouts barely caught the attention of the rampaging demons. "Guys! Hey! I didn't invite you lot to the scrapyard so you could eat me out of house and home. Get off the scrap, all of you! The Priestess of Cerridwen has a boon to ask of you."

Finally, the largest of the ferrous demons cocked his head, his luminous green eyes gazing at Carb thoughtfully. Then his gaze moved to Cerri, standing calmly next to Carb in the center of the forecourt.

The SBI agent wore the flowing white robes associated with her priestess role. In her right hand, she grasped a tall ritual staff, its crystal tip wreathed in the iridescent blue power of her patron goddess.

The massive demon eyed Cerri's staff, then dipped his head

respectfully. He climbed down off his chosen mound and loped into the forecourt, where he beat his fists on an empty metal drum, the booming sound echoing in the night air.

Once the drum beater had the attention of the other demons, he shouted, "Alright, everyone! The scrap metal potluck is off. Get your thickheaded asses down here. Now."

One by one, the demons reluctantly ended their feasting and descended from the metal mountains.

As the last of the demons loped into the forecourt, the large demon who had given the command nodded in satisfaction, then turned and bowed to Cerri. "Priestess of Cerridwen, Hail and Welcome. My name is Astetes. Please forgive my subordinates. They have the manners of a bunch of hell-monkeys, which is to say, absolutely none."

By the end of Astetes' speech, the demons behind him had formed a precise line and stood at attention. As one, they bowed to Cerri and shouted, "Priestess of Cerridwen. Hail and Welcome. How may we serve you?"

Larry whispered to Carb, "What a bunch of brown-nosers. Takes a powerful witch like Cerri to get that lot to behave. No wonder you never invited any of these yahoos over."

Carb snickered softly.

"I heard that." Astetes threw Carb and Larry a sneer, his lips curled in disdain.

Cerri patted the air and gave her audience a no-nonsense glare. "Gentlemen, ladies, now is not the time for bickering. The world, indeed, the galaxy is in imminent danger, as are all the supernatural realms, including your original home in the Underworld. Without your help, we will all lose everything we hold dear, including our lives and those of our loved ones."

Her stern gaze traveled over the assembled demons. "We have invited you here tonight to request your help prevent this ultimate destruction, so listen up. There is a cosmos-ending astro-magical machine called the Universum hidden within this scrapyard. Its Guardian hid the Universum well and placed wards of great power around it. While crafted mainly of base metal, the machine also features gold and silver components. As ferrous demons, metal is your specialty. Your unique magical powers can sense this dangerous machine and will locate it more quickly than my witch team."

She hesitated, before glancing down at Midnight, who bowed her head and mewed plaintively. "Without your help, a good man will soon give his life to protect the location of the Universum. However, his sacrifice will only delay the inevitable. The evil mages torturing this man will not stop until they have the Universum in their hands."

Astetes rubbed his chin and grinned slyly. "While I understand your predicament, Priestess, if I may be so bold as to ask, what's in it for us?"

Cerri gave the smug demon a steely smile, her eyes flashing with intensity. "What's in it for you? Simply put: if you help us, you will all get to live. If you don't, you and every single one of your kind will die. If the Universum falls into the wrong hands, its activation will obliterate every planet, star, realm, and living thing within a billion miles—and we are running out of time to prevent that catastrophe."

After her bald statement, Cerri paused, and a tense silence reigned. She let the silence lengthen, giving the assembled demons time to digest the import of her words.

Carb shared a mind-spoken observation with Larry and Cerri. *"I think you've got most of 'em on your side, Cerri, but ferrous demons are a proud and selfish bunch. I suggest you make a formal plea for their help. That'll appeal to their ego and should do the trick."*

Cerri flicked a subtle glance at Carb and gave him a slight nod. She dipped her chin at the assembled demons and bound them with praise and portent. "Noble ferrous demons, will you kindly help us by using your unsurpassed metal magic skills to locate this infernal machine? If we can rely on your superior assistance to find the Universum, my team can concentrate on rescuing the machine's Guardian and defeating those who seek to steal and activate it, despite the dire consequences. If you—or we don't succeed, we are all doomed."

The gathered demons stood in silence, their inward gazes reflecting a mind-conversation to which Cerri, Larry, and Carb were not privy. Larry tried not to fidget as they waited for the demon's answer. After several tense minutes, Astetes gave Cerri a nod of affirmation. Larry couldn't help woofing in gratitude. Beside him, Carb raised a fist in the air and grinned triumphantly at his fellow demons.

Cerri gave Astetes a regal nod of thanks before turning her gaze to the small demon at her side. "As the scrapyard is your domain, Carb, I'm placing you in charge of the search. Please report directly to Larry or me with your team's progress."

Carb's shoulders rose, and a faint yellow blush colored his green cheeks. "Yes, ma'am. I—we will do our best." He shot an interrogatory glance at Astetes. "Right?"

The larger demon's lips pursed in displeasure at the usurpation of his command, but he nodded in reluctant agreement. He gestured at the demons behind him and shouted, "Let's get to work, folks, before a bunch of conniving fools destroy everything."

THAT SHIP HASN'T SAILED

Water slapped against the dock's slick wooden surface a mere twenty yards from their hiding place. Sharp scents of brine and diesel oil filtered through the many cracks in the storage shack's dilapidated walls.

Half buried by weeds at the edge of the defunct marina's cracked asphalt parking lot, the rotting wooden shack offered cramped cover to the surveillance team as they observed the oversized yacht secured to the far side of the dock.

Larry covered his nose with his paws and smothered a sneeze. "Geeze, this place stinks."

"Shhhh." Risa hissed a whispered rebuke. "They probably have Air witches listening for intruders."

It was their second night spent spying on the disused marina. Sandwiched between two brand new, modern marinas in Bridgeport Harbor, where sleek yachts bobbed next to shiny metal docks, the run-down boatyard and its barnacle-covered wooden dock appeared abandoned ... except for the fancy vessel moored to the dilapidated dock.

After two nights of surveillance, the SBI team and Larry

had a better idea of their rescue task—and it would't be easy. Armed men patrolled the ship's extensive walkways and the dock. Half a dozen mages made regular appearances on deck, while a shiny black limousine had made several ominous visits, gliding into the parking lot at random times. At least two bodyguards always accompanied the heavyset, muscular man who emerged from the vehicle. Risa had confirmed the man was Michael Malfisco, the magical mobster who coveted the Universum. He never stayed long, but the growing frustration on his face each time he left had the rescue team worried.

Midnight visited the surveillance shed each night, reaching out to her magical partner through their mind link. She sighed in despair after her latest attempt. "I can tell Ted's still alive, but he's very weak. He can no longer speak, not even in his mind."

She paused and shook her head, dread filling her eyes. "For the first time, I can sense another presence in his mind. To have broken Ted's mind wards like that, its gotta be a powerful Air Witch. The asshole is rifling through Ted's surface memories, but he hasn't yet been able to unlock the wards guarding Ted's closest secrets. I helped Ted build those wards, so those suckers are mega-strong ... but they're not impenetrable." Urgency colored her next words. "We have little time to rescue Ted before he, um, well, you know."

"Gives up the location of the Universum, albeit unwillingly, or ...." Larry paused, hesitating to verbalize what they all feared.

"He dies," Midnight whispered, her expression resigned. "He won't be the first Guardian I've lost, but he might just be the last, if we lose control of the Universum."

A morose silence overtook the watchers.

The strident cries of seagulls pierced the night air, the grey and white birds wheeling and diving as they sought a last meal and a suitable spot to roost for the night.

Everyone in the shed knew they would have to attempt their rescue mission soon, no matter what. Hopefully, by then, the ferrous demons would have located the Universum, so Ted and Midnight could spirit the infernal thing away from the scrapyard ... and hide it better next time.

AFTER MUCH DISCUSSION, the team agreed upon a rescue plan. Larry had a bad feeling about it, but couldn't come up with a better plan, so he was on board. He would not lie low and ignore danger to those in his circle ever again.

That night, with cloudy skies hiding the moon, the most powerful members of the SBI team, along with Larry and Midnight, launched their rescue mission. They had waited until well after midnight, when the guards were operating on a skeleton crew and there was less chance of Michael, or any other magical heavy hitters, being on board.

During their final preparations, Cerri received word from her sources at the Boston SBI that Litha had been confirmed present at a Witch Council dinner in Salem. There had been no recent sightings of Councilman Jenkins, but Larry didn't think the corrupt councilman would miss attending a Witch Council dinner with his attractive co-conspirator. The traitorous pair should be hundreds of miles away from the boatyard during the rescue operation.

The mission required precision and excellent coordination between the witches on the team. Risa's excellent skills as a Water witch were critical, since she could power her magic using the water surrounding the ship. Once on board, Cerri's skills as an Earth witch would come into their own, as the vessel's wooden and metal surfaces were Earth elements.

The team members had been chosen with care, with their magical specialties and strengths in mind. It was a strong team, but there were too many variables to predict the outcome of their rescue mission.

Larry sighed. Talk about a perfect place to use as a hideout and prisoner stash house ... on a ship that straddled so many different elements. Especially if you knew those pursuing you were Elemental witches.

RISA WAS the first to act. She quietly slipped down to the water at the edge of the dock. Her job was to use her powerful Water magic to 'freeze' the water surrounding the vessel. This would prevent the bad guys from moving the ship away from the dock and taking it into open waters outside the harbor.

Larry watched in awe as Risa poured the contents of a small vial into the water while whispering an incantation. Within seconds, the water around the ship jelled into an ice-like slush, then froze solid, encasing the hull in a cold, crystalline prison. *Goddess, that Risa was one powerful Water witch*, he mused.

A shadow slipped by Larry's peripheral vision. He squinted in the darkness, even his excellent canine eyes having trouble identifying the team leader.

Cerri was almost invisible, her Earth magic obscuring her body as she waved the team forward with a mind-spoken command. *"Hurry up, everyone! The guards are patrolling on the far side of the main cabin. Time to board!"*

Larry and the others silently traversed the slippery dock and swarmed up the ladder and onto the vessel's deck. Each team member knew their assignment and split off from the group to undertake their missions. Assigned to Ted's rescue, Larry and Midnight peeled away toward the under-deck stairs. Before they had travelled more than a few yards, the night air lit up with shouts and gunfire.

Arrows flaming with magical fire thudded into the deck behind Larry. He swerved and glanced over his shoulder, where he spotted several bad guys racing toward their position. *"Shit,*

Midnight! They were ready for us. There must be a mole on our team. Go find Ted and get him out of here!" Larry mind-spoke his command at the black cat, then charged into battle for the fight of his life.

Cries of pain, accompanied by blasts of magic, and gunfire filled the night air. The deck rumbled as someone started the ship's huge motors. Risa, still stationed on the dock below, mind-screamed to the team, *"I won't let them take the fight away from the dock. I'll make sure the ice holds!"*

~

LARRY DEFEATED several mages with his powerful magic, leaving them unconscious on the deck.

When a furry missile hit him hard in the flank and claws raked at his face, he stumbled into the ship's guardrail. Only his massive junkyard dog size prevented him from falling overboard. He rebounded off the hard metal rail, snapping his jaws at his attacker, but his muscular bulk left him at a disadvantage against the lithe frenzy of his feline assailant.

"Cleo! What the hell are you doing here!" Larry barked, shocked at seeing Litha's new Familiar on the ship, hundreds of miles away from her magical partner. His distraction left him open to a razor-like swat from Cleo's quick claws. "Ouch! You damn cat! What are you doing here? You're supposed to be in Salem with your magical partner."

Cleo's smug smile made Larry's blood run cold. "I'm not attached at the hip to Litha, dog-breath. In fact, I'm not attached to that narcissistic witch at all." The traitorous cat flicked a glance over her shoulder and purred, "My chosen partner is here with me tonight, defending our right to a place on the Universum mission."

Larry's eyes followed Cleo's, and his eyes widened in shock.

So much for his wishful thinking that Councilman Jenkins would be at Litha's side for the Witch Council dinner. Sigh.

The corrupt councilman approached the pair of Familiars, his arctic eyes and curved lips revealing malicious pleasure at Larry's dismay. He ran his hand over Cleo's head and the cat purred loudly, arching her back in pleasure. "That's right, Larry. Cleo and I have teamed up. She has chosen to be my Familiar and is here at my side, in her rightful place as my magical partner."

Larry knew it didn't work like that. Familiars could not choose their magical partners. He turned a confused gaze on the triumphant cat at the councilman's side. "But what about Litha, Cleo? You told me DEAF appointed you as her High Familiar—"

"I lied. In fact, I lied a lot." Cleo's green eyes gleamed, and she chuckled in amusement. "I haven't spoken with DEAF in years—not since they assigned me to that magical wet noodle, Jesse. As far as DEAF is concerned, I'm still assigned as Jesse's Familiar."

Oblivious to the ongoing battle in other parts of the ship, Larry sat on the deck and stared at Cleo in shock. "But how ... you told me DEAF had appointed me as Jesse's new Familiar after Mabel's death, since Litha wanted you instead of me. As the coven's new High Priestess, she could request a High Familiar of her choice."

A sick understanding filled Larry's mind. "Burt. That conniving toad is still her Familiar, isn't he? She didn't plan to sacrifice him at her ascendance ritual at all."

Cleo snickered. "Of course not. Burt's a good toad, and completely loyal to Litha. I only told you that Litha was going to sacrifice him and that she didn't want you to take his place as High Familiar to get you and Jesse together. We knew you two would try to investigate Mabel's death, which would give us good cause to get you both kicked out of the coven and out of our way."

Larry frowned as he tried to put all the pieces together. "Is Litha even involved in the Universum plot at all? Or is she just your garden variety murdering bitch witch who wanted her own coven and killed Mabel to get it?"

"Does it really matter?" The councilman answered for Cleo, his hard gaze focused on Larry. "You and your compatriots failed in your rescue mission today. Soon, the wards protecting the scrapyard will fall and the Universum will be ours."

"It matters," Larry growled. "Was ... is Litha involved in the Universum plot? Did she kill Mabel so she could take over the coven with your help? Yes or no answers, if you please."

Councilman Jenkins grinned and replied offhandedly. "Well then, yes, Litha is in it up to her pretty little neck. The only reason she's not here tonight is so she can give herself an alibi and put the SBI off her scent. We know she's under observation. To answer your other question: yes, she killed the old bat so she could take over her coven. We'll need a coven-full of witches with decent magic where we're going ... with the Universum's help."

THE COUNCILMAN'S LEVEL WORDS, with their arrogant assurance of success, spurred Larry into action. He pulled hard at his power until a rich golden glow covered his fur. Gleaming tendrils of magic whipped off his body and swirled, snakelike, across the ship's deck.

Closing his eyes, he pinpointed the location of each team member and sent the magical lifelines to them. He mind-shouted a command, *"Everyone, grab the nearest magical lifeline! I'm gonna pull us all into a ley line!"*

He stumbled as the team heeded his urgent call. His

magical power stretched thin, but he held tight to each lifeline as Cerri's mind-scream echoed in his head. *"Now, Larry! The ship is pulling away from the dock!"*

Giving a shocked Cleo one last glance, Larry dived over the railing and onto the dock's slick surface, his massive paws pounding towards the shoreline. *Here goes nothing.*

Seconds later, he reached solid ground. He sucked in a breath, leapt into the air, braced himself for the pain he knew would come, and dived straight toward the parking lot's cracked asphalt.

With a final mighty pull on his magic, Larry ripped open a tunnel into the ley line he knew lay directly underneath the abandoned marina's paved surface. He howled in agony, and used the last of his magic to pull his team members into the ley line with him.

As Larry entered the ley line's flowing magical river, the last thing he heard was Cerri shouting, "They have Risa! She couldn't break free!" *Oh, shit.*

17

WAKEY, WAKEY

The annoying buzzing sound was getting louder. Larry frowned in annoyance and covered his ears with his paws. A gentle hand removed one paw and stroked his head. The buzzing sound soon turned into words.

"Larry? Larry, honey, please wake up. Please be okay. I promise I'll never not listen to you again. Please wake up, bud." Jesse's soft pleas continued as she smoothed Larry's fur and gently massaged his ears.

His magical partner's words receded into the babble of voices murmuring in the background. Larry lost focus, his mind begging to return to the oblivion of sleep.

"Alright, lazy ass, get your lazy butt out of that bed. Wakey, wakey, rise and shine! We've got work to do, kibble-breath." Midnight's brassy mind-spoken command rattled around in Larry's brain, forcing his eyes open. He gazed blearily at Jesse, seated on the bed beside him. Midnight, perched on the pillow above his head, gazed down at him in concern.

Yawning widely, Larry shook his head. "Wassup, everyone? Why the long faces?" Then he remembered. Shots and screams, icy betrayal, and a desperate escape. By jumping into a ley line mid-stream, instead of using a Crossroads, and bringing half a dozen others with him, he had maxed out his magic and done something very few Familiars could do. It was a miracle that he ... and his team members, had lived through the experience.

He sat up gingerly, his gaze bouncing between Jesse's tearful face and Midnight's worried eyes. "Did ... did we lose anyone?"

Midnight jerked her head to the right, whiskers aimed at Larry's far side. Feeling the bed dip as someone sat behind him, Larry scrambled around to face the new arrival.

"Hello Larry. Welcome back." Cerri's outwardly calm demeanor belied the swirling mix of emotions in her eyes.

"First, let me take this opportunity to thank you on behalf of the SBI and the goddess Cerridwen for your heroic actions. If you had not used your considerable magical power to save us by doing something I have never seen done before—and that I'm not even sure DEAF knows you can do—our team would surely have suffered more losses."

Dread filled Larry, curdling his stomach. "More losses? Who did we lose?"

Cerri's gaze met his steadily as she replied, "I'm afraid Risa remained behind. She had to keep using her magic, so the ice around the ship remained frozen, holding the vessel in place. Unfortunately, several powerful Fire mages were on board that night, and they fought to counter her water magic."

Her eyes darkened in remembrance. "When you jumped off the ship, you must have noticed the steam coming from the melting ice, as well as the flames all around the dock." She shook her head and sighed deeply. "Risa did what she had to do: she stayed behind to give the rest of us a chance to escape."

Larry swallowed thickly. "Is she ...?"

The SBI agent mustered up a small smile. "Risa was injured and captured, but she's still alive. As both her supervisor and her good friend, I can mind link with her over great distances.

She tells me she's now imprisoned with Ted, which is a good thing. They can support each other until we rescue them both."

He flicked a worried the others in the room and mind-spoke a request to Cerri, which he shared with Jesse. *"Uh, can we leave the bit about me jumping into a ley-line mid-stream, without using a Crossroads—and bringing company with me—out of the official report? What DEAF and the Supernatural Council don't know won't hurt anyone ... me in particular, okay?"*

Jesse and Cerri shared a silent look, then both smiled affectionately at Larry.

Cerri gave him an almost imperceptible nod and mind-spoke her reply. *"We have already submitted the official report. There is no mention of your unusual magical ability, my friend. The report simply states that we made a strategic retreat from the target location once it was clear the bad guys were expecting us."*

Jesse nodded at Larry, a conspiratorial smile hovering on her lips. *"Your secret is safe with us, bud."*

Larry heaved a sigh of relief and shared mind-spoken words of gratitude with his two friends. *"Thanks, guys. I really appreciate your help."*

LARRY ROSE UNSTEADILY to his feet and shook himself from nose to tail. "Speaking of help, we have a rescue mission to plan. Who's with me? I'm done with coasting along and ignoring my gut when it tells me something's wrong and that my friends need my help." Ears drooping as his thoughts turned to Mabel, his murdered magical partner, he snorted and reiterated, "I'm so done with that crap."

"Not so fast, you feisty Familiar," Cerri cautioned with a grin. "It's great that you're primed and ready for action to protect those around you from danger. And thank you again for your valiant efforts in doing just that the other day. But wouldn't it be better to have a plan to improve your—our chances of success?"

Larry's eyes widened. "The other day? How long have I been out?"

Jesse replied tersely, "Over twenty-four hours."

"Holy shit! There's no time to waste!" Larry tried to leap off the bed, but Cerri placed a restraining hand on his collar.

"Slow down, Larry. Sit down and listen to me, please," Cerri cautioned.

Reluctantly, Larry complied. "Okay, okay. I'm sitting. And listening. Now what?"

Cerri's lips curved into a scheming smile. "Now, you listen. While you've been napping and recovering your strength, the rest of us have been planning. Remember, Familiar, while it's good that you're now committed to proactively working to protect those around you, it might also be wise to consider trusting those same individuals to help you as well."

Larry glumly considered his earlier decision to trust Mabel's assurances that there was no real danger lurking in the coven. "But I think I've been too trusting in the past and haven't been paying enough attention to, well ... everything. That's what got us into this mess in the first place."

His spirits dipped even further when he recalled Cleo's smirking face the night of their aborted rescue mission.

Midnight padded over and brushed her silky body down Larry's side before returning to her perch on the pillow. "Listen, numbnuts. I'm sure you've heard the expression trust ... but verify. How about the one that goes there's no I in team? Personally, I think the second saying is corny as hell, but both fit this situation."

The small cat's chest rumbled with an impatient purr. "Yes, you need to trust those in your circle, but you also need to pay attention to your gut. That's your biggest failing right there. Not lack of courage, that's for sure. Listening to your gut and using that knowledge to ensure those around you are both deserving of your trust and safe are your best bet, Larry. You really do need to have faith in yourself and in those around you who prove worthy."

Fixing Larry with serious eyes, Midnight mind-spoke a caution, *"Remember this, dog ... you are not responsible for other's poor decisions, or even their betrayal. Mabel chose not to share the danger she suspected with you. Cleo chose to betray your trust—and that of the coven."*

Larry bit back a protest as the truth of Midnight's words settled in his heart. If only he could get his head on board with the cat's wise words, he'd be good.

"So, what's the plan, guys? And how can I help?" Larry's determined gaze scanned the faces of those gathered around him.

18

FAMILIAR FRIENDS ... AND ENEMIES

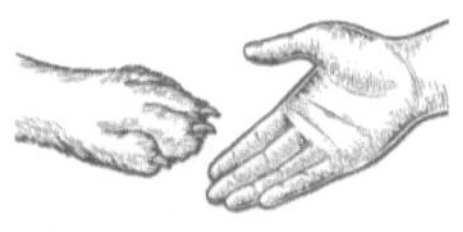

"Holy crap, you guys have been busy!" Larry stared wide-eyed at Cerri after she finished updating him on everything that had happened while he recovered from his magical burnout.

Cerri nodded in confirmation and added, "Oh, and the ferrous demons have narrowed down the location of the Universum and estimate they'll identify the final protections around it shortly."

Larry shook his head, muzzle open in wonder. Then his gaze turned soft, and he peered up at Jesse, still sitting by his side in silent support. "Is what Cerri says true, Jess? You guys contacted DEAF, explained what's been going on, and asked to make our bond official ... and they agreed to it?"

"Yep. It's done. You're officially stuck with me as your magical partner, bud," Jesse replied with a grin. Then she winced and gave him an apologetic look. "Um, I just wanted to tell you it's my fault the rescue mission failed. Since Cleo was still my Familiar, she could access my thoughts and I ... well, I just didn't notice. That's how the bad guys found out about the rescue mission, and why they were ready for us."

Her eyes welled with tears as she reached a tentative hand out to pet Larry's head. "I'm so sorry, Larry. I should have known that Cleo was lying when she told you she'd been officially reassigned to Litha. Speaking of not trusting your gut, I'm as guilty of it as you are." With a shrug, she added, "Cleo's always been power hungry. We had many battles over the years about my supposed lack of ambition."

Larry nuzzled his head into his new magical partner's hand, appreciating the fact that she knew just the place to scratch behind his ears to get his back leg going. "What'll happen to Cleo now? Once we catch her, I mean," he asked. "It's almost unheard of for a Familiar to go rogue, betray their magical partner, and unilaterally align themselves with another supernatural." His eyes narrowed in anger at the memory of Cleo standing defiantly by Councilman Jenkins' side as the battle on the ship raged around them.

Jesse snickered and shook her head. "Oh, Cleo's in for a world of hurt. DEAF told us they are going to recall her, once this is over. At the least, she'll have to go for intensive retraining. At worst—"

Larry nodded in understanding. "At worst, they'll deconstruct her soul." He shuddered in horror. Deconstruction was rumored to be excruciatingly painful and bloody. And, at the end of it, you were no more, ever again.

Grim silence filled the room as everyone pondered Cleo's grisly fate.

～

MIDNIGHT ROSE rose from her comfortable perch on the pillow at the head of the bed and arched her back, chittering impatiently. "Deconstruction is exactly what that traitorous creature deserves. But why haven't they recalled her yet? Why are they leaving her in place with that idiot councilman?" Her eyes widened, and she breathed, "... oh, I think I get it."

Cerri grinned evilly. "I requested that DEAF leave Cleo in place AND keep her technically assigned to Jesse as her Familiar for the time being, and they agreed. Some witches do have more than one Familiar, so this doesn't interfere with Larry's assignment to Jesse at all."

Larry stared admiringly at the wily—and obviously well-connected SBI agent. "Soooo, since Jesse is still technically partnered with Cleo, she can access Cleo's thoughts, just like that damn cat did to Jesse when she mentally eavesdropped and discovered our rescue plan, right?"

Jesse and Cerri exchanged a triumphant grin. At Cerri's urging, Jesse explained. "You're a fast learner, Larry. Cerri has placed a magi-block on my mind so that Cleo can only access a loop of pre-planned surface thoughts. You know ... about how worried I am about you and about the scrapyard. That kind of thing. But she can't access anything deeper than that. We don't want to alert her to the fact that we know about her accessing my thoughts by blocking her completely because—"

Cerri picked up the explanation, her eyes twinkling with mischief. "We don't want Cleo to know she's been found out because two can play at the mind-access game, Larry. From what I can tell, Cleo has always underestimated Jesse's magical and mental abilities. If we leave Jesse's surface thoughts open to Cleo, and keep them routine, she won't suspect that Jesse has discovered her magical mind spying. We're hoping it won't occur to Cleo that Jesse can return the favor."

Larry's eyes widened at the implications of Cerri's words. "That means, if she's careful, and doesn't probe too far or too much, Jesse has a direct line into Cleo's mess of a mind, and the cat won't know it, right? And, since that damned cat has aligned herself with Councilman Jenkins and he's in league with the magical mobster hunting the Universum, we'll have a pretty good idea of his plans as well." He gazed proudly between Cerri and Jesse, and exclaimed, "That's just brilliant, you two!"

Cerri smiled and nodded her thanks at his praise. "Keeping a magical eye on Cleo's thoughts will benefit us. However, we are going to need a lot more help to have any chance of saving the scrapyard and protecting the Universum. I'm afraid we ... I have drastically underestimated the scope of this plot."

She rubbed her eyes tiredly and shook her head. "There are way more bad actors involved in this than we expected, Larry. Plus, Risa's discovery that the mage mobster, Michael Malfisco, is the one who kidnapped Ted and is after the Universum ups the danger quotient exponentially."

Jesse gave Larry a worried look. "The bad guys have more bodies and thus more magical firepower than we do. We're going to need reinforcements, if we want to have any chance of beating them and saving ourselves—and, well, the galaxy and everything else."

19

FAMILIAR REINFORCEMENTS

Later that evening, the cramped scrapyard office heaved with furred and feathered creatures.

"So, who's on board?" Midnight asked as she gazed around the room, ensuring she met the eyes of every Familiar present. "Like I just said, we can't have Familiars going rogue. Cleo's actions have damaged our standing with the Supernatural Council and alerted DEAF to a betrayal by one of our own. DEAF will clamp down on the small amount of autonomy us Familiars are allowed ... and it won't be pleasant."

The gathered Familiars eyed each other and shifted uneasily. Claws clicked on the office's hardwood floor, while beaks clacked and feathers ruffled, heightening the already tense atmosphere.

Earlier that day, DEAF had issued a call to action to all Familiars closest to the scrapyard, commanding them to leave their posts and report for duty. By sunset, the scrapyard's office was stuffed to the gills with Familiars from all over the Tri-State region. A battle for survival was brewing, and these Familiars knew it, although hesitation still reflected on several faces.

Midnight mind-spoke her doubts to Larry. *"You really think anyone in this motley crew is brave enough to be of any help? I just don't see it myself."*

Larry flicked an irritated side-eye at his feline friend, then gazed around the room, wondering the same thing. He needed to make the Familiars listen—even if they didn't want to. "Listen up, everyone. Cleo betrayed the Familiar Oath we all take. You know, the one that binds us to assist and protect our magical partners. Instead, she conspired against Jesse, then lied about it and aligned herself with those who plan to destroy everything in their mad quest for power."

Finishing his speech with a philosophical shrug, he added, "The way DEAF sees it, if one Familiar can do something like that, so can the rest of us. The way I see it is that we must band together—both to save ourselves and the galaxy from this existential threat AND to regain our collective honor."

His gaze remained serious as he scanned faces around the room, hoping his rousing speech did the trick. "Who is with us?" He barked.

After several tense moments, a large beaver lumbered forward, his flat tail leaving a trail of dirt on the formerly pristine office floor. The heavyset creature sat up on his hind legs, his lugubrious face swiveling between Larry and Midnight. "We get it, guys. Us Familiars have no choice but to save the day. Yet again."

The beaver's tail slapped angrily against the wooden floor. "Don't these supernaturals ever consider our needs? Our wants? Granted, we Familiars were created to provide magical support to our supernatural partners, but what's actually in it for us? We go where we're told, work with whatever magical loser DEAF assigns us to, and when—not if—but when we lose our physical body in service to the supernatural community, we're just shoved into another body and sent on yet another assignment. Rinse and repeat." The beaver subsided into silence, but his frustration pulsed in the air.

Larry noted that several heads in the room had nodded in agreement during the beaver's aggrieved speech, so he dropped a truth bomb. Despite appearances, his gut told him that every Familiar present, even the not-so-eager beaver, would eventually agree to do their oath-bound duty and help him—and his team, save the galaxy.

"Look guys, I get it. I really do. I'm pretty sure I'm the oldest Familiar here. I've been … uh … recycled well over a dozen times." Larry gestured at his massive and heavily muscled canine body with a wry grin. "Unfortunately, not all my physical forms have been as impressive as this one. And don't even ask me about my gigs spent as a cat." He shuddered and rolled his eyes dramatically.

"Hey! Watch it, dog-face!" Several annoyed feline protests rose above the general guffaws of the audience.

The tense atmosphere in the room lightened, as Larry had intended. "Overall, though, my many lives spent as a Familiar never cease to amaze me. Thanks to DEAF, I get to experience the sun on my face and the exhilaration of working powerful magic with, mostly, great magical partners. I get to enjoy good food and good friends. Most of all, I get to live."

His enquiring gaze raked the room. "How many of you would rather never have been created—never have experienced any of those things?"

After an electric moment, the rafters shook with roars, meows, woofs, and caws of agreement. Once the din died down, Larry faced his chief opponent in the battle for hearts and minds. "Well? How about you? It can't be so bad being a beaver." Larry couldn't help himself, adding, "Well, except for all the beaver jokes."

"Oh, screw you, dog breath!" The beaver shouted and shook a clenched paw at Larry. Then his shoulders drooped and he reluctantly agreed. "But you're right, dammit. I'm glad to be alive. Without DEAF and the supernatural community, I wouldn't be. I'll help you. We'll all help you, right, folks?" The beaver glared at the other Familiars, a challenge in his eyes, then grumbled, "But quit it with the beaver jokes, guys."

Turning to Larry, the beaver extended his paw. "By the way, my name's Ed. I'm in, and so are the rest of these yahoos. Let us know how we can help."

"Nice to meet you, Ed," Larry replied, suppressing a sigh of relief as he touched paws with the now cooperative beaver.

Amid a chorus of hoots and hollers, they had agreed. The gathered Familiars would stand beside Larry and Midnight, and the rest of their team, in the coming battle to save the galaxy.

As the Familiars chatted eagerly amongst themselves, Midnight's caustic, mind-spoken comment sounded in Larry's head. *"Good job—for a canine."*

"You, too—for a cat," he replied.

20

———

SCRAPYARD SKIRMISH

Once Larry and Midnight had secured the Familiars' agreement, Jesse and Cerri and her team joined the meeting in the overflowing office. Cerri spent over an hour briefing the Familiars on the plans to rescue the hostages, defeat the bad guys, and save the galaxy.

"Does anyone have questions?" Cerri asked after finishing her briefing. As Larry expected, Ed the Beaver was the first to raise his paw. Ed's question was drowned out when a magical missile blew out the office's front window, raining fire and glass on those gathered within.

Larry threw Jesse a what-the-hell look. She gave him the finger. After that, they were too busy trying to stay alive to communicate much.

Cerri's shouted commands sent everyone scurrying. "Familiars, exit through the back door and fan out along the perimeter. Use your magic to reinforce the wards. Pull on my Earth power, if you need to. Team members protect the scrapyard's main access points and assist the Familiars if needed. Jesse, Larry ... stay with me."

Once everyone else had raced out of the office, intent on their assigned tasks, Cerri pulled a small bottle from her pocket and smashed it on the office floor. Sizzling steam spiraled from the broken glass and a deafening boom echoed in the small space. Then the ground heaved as ripples of powerful Earth magic rattled the floorboards. Larry stumbled and fell, narrowly avoiding a fiery arrow that came sailing through the front window's shattered glass. "Ow, what the hell?" He barked.

The magical earthquake Cerri had started quickly spread outward, rolling across the scrapyard's dusty ground until it passed under the fence. Metal fenceposts heaved but remained standing, while the fencing flexed but held firm, as did the wards.

Once outside the wards, the earthquake intensified with a powerful roar. The earth bucked and buckled under the attackers; their shouts and screams competed with the earthquake's deep rumble.

Taking advantage of the lull in battle, Cerri hustled Larry and Jesse out of the office, and the trio took cover behind the nearest metal mountain. The SBI agent gave them a hard look and told them to stay safe before racing off to join her team.

In the silent seconds after Cerri left, Jesse met Larry's eyes, hers a mix of disappointment, determination, and fear. "Cleo must not have known about tonight's attack. I was just listening in on her mind an hour ago, and there was nothing there ... well, aside from the usual feline nonsense."

"I'd bet that Cleo and her corrupt councilman headed to Boston to meet up with Litha after the fight at the marina," Larry replied. "If that's the case, they almost certainly weren't aware of tonight's raid, which explains why you didn't find any thoughts about it in Cleo's mind."

Jesse's tense shoulders eased at Larry's words. "You're probably right, bud. I just worry, you know? I'm doing the best I can." She inhaled deeply, then blew out a calming breath before giving Larry a determined look. "So, what do we do now, fur-face?"

"Now, we fight," Larry replied. He stood and pulled hard on his magic until it writhed around his muscular body, the power's deep golden glow highlighting shards of shiny metal mixed in with the rusted scrap heap. "Touch my fur, Jesse, and stock up on my power. Let's give these idiots something to scream about."

Long hours later, as the first pink rays of dawn colored the horizon, the battle ended. Half a dozen metal mountains lay in ruins, now just mere hills that ran together in a twisted, magic-darkened pile of destruction.

Exhausted Familiars left their battle positions along the perimeter, carefully skirting the sharp metal and glass shards littering the ground, before gathering on the forecourt. Cerri and her team followed the Familiars, before sprawling on the ground near the office, chests heaving with exhaustion. After circuiting the perimeter to ensure the wards held, Jesse and Larry staggered toward the office, then collapsed onto a patch of weeds near the office's back steps.

Into the dawn's silence, morning birds twittered, heralding the new day. When a raspy throat cleared, Larry leapt to his feet, raking the area with a fierce gaze, his magic glowing gold in the early morning light.

"Peace, Larry!" Carb shouted as he emerged near the top of one of the few remaining metal mountains. His small, agile form clambered quickly to the ground before scampering across the forecourt. "It's only me. Glad the battle's over, but you guys sure made a mess." The ferrous demon gazed sadly at the destruction. "And just when I had everything so nicely arranged, too."

Larry let his magic recede; Carb was no threat, despite his insinuation that the scrapyard's dire condition was his team's fault. "In case you didn't notice, Carb, the bad guys attacked us. They're the ones responsible for the mess. Not us."

Carb grinned slyly at his new friend. "But you helped."

With a reluctant snicker, Larry nodded. "Yes. We helped."

After a last pained glance at the metal mayhem strewn across the scrapyard, Carb straightened, faced Cerri, and issued a sharp salute. "Hail, Priestess of Cerridwen. I have a progress report on my demon team's search for the Universum." He grimaced and added, "Oh, and I figured you guys had the bad guys under control, so I kept my team on task—seeking the Universum. I assume I did the right thing?"

Cerri had brightened during Carb's speech, her former tired slump gone. "You did the right thing, Carb. Tell me what you have discovered."

Carb hesitated, his eyes roving over the few witches and Familiars still resting nearby. Almost everyone else was working to repair the scrapyard fencing and providing first aid to the injured. A few had drawn the short straw and were busy clearing away the remnants of the battle outside the gates, carefully avoiding the deep crevices that now stretched greedy fingers around the fence's perimeter. Cerri's magical earthquake had been a humdinger.

Correctly interpreting the reason for Carb's hesitation, Cerri told the little demon that everyone within hearing distance was trustworthy, so he could speak freely. Carb nodded in understanding, then straightened and gave Cerri another salute.

"My team has located the quadrant containing the Universum, ma'am." He aimed a respectful nod at Midnight and added, "I must compliment you, Familiar. You and your partner did an admirable job of hiding and warding the blasted thing."

Midnight's whiskers twitched with pleasure. "Why thank you, Carb."

"Just one question ... well, two, really." Carb waited for Midnight to blink her agreement before he asked, "Um ... since you are the big deal Felinus Universum, how come you didn't know the Universum's exact location in the scrapyard? Or did you? And if you knew, why did you ask me and the other ferrous demons to spend days hunting for the damn thing?" The little demon scuffed his feet in the dirt. "You lot weren't just giving us busy work, were you?"

Midnight licked her paw and ran it over her ear and down her muzzle. She continued her grooming session, concentrating on a patch of dirt entangled in the fur behind her left ear. After several uncomfortable minutes of silence, during which Larry wondered if the regal feline would deign to answer Carb's quite legitimate question, she ceased her obsessive grooming and sat up straight, her two front paws in perfect alignment and deigned to provide an answer.

"My magical partner and I are bound by a Life Oath never to reveal the location of the Universum on pain of final death." Midnight sighed deeply and gave a sad meow. "That's why Ted hasn't told his kidnappers where the damn thing is, no matter how much they torture him. He can't tell them, or he'll lose not just his life, but his soul will be snuffed out of existence! The same goes for me."

Larry cringed in sympathy at Midnight's and Ted's deadly magical obligation. Their continued existence was bound to a tool of cosmic destruction.

Carb squatted, bringing his gaze level with Midnight's. "Thank you for sharing the truth with me, Familiar." He dipped his head respectfully. "I understand now. My sincerest apologies for questioning your honor. You have helped us as much as you can, risking your very soul to do so."

Larry caught Midnight's fleeting expression of pleasure, even if the others didn't. Mere seconds later, her normal inscrutable expression blanketed her face, and she merely dipped her chin to acknowledge Carb's words of praise.

ONCE THE DEFENDERS had cleaned up after the battle, they quickly disbursed, many retiring to the main house to rest. Others patrolled the perimeter, while Cerri huddled with her SBI team, deep in conversation. Jesse had insisted on helping with the cleanup, despite her exhaustion. She had only retreated to her room to rest after Larry badgered her into doing so.

The promise of the dawn had given way to a cloudy morning. Rain fell intermittently from the gray sky overhead. While small shards of metal and glass still littered the forecourt's cracked asphalt, someone had neatly boarded up the office's damaged front window and wedged the front door into its frame.

Larry gingerly pushed his head through the cat flap in the damaged door and checked out the office's dim interior. The kitten nursery under the desk was cold and empty. After the battle, Midnight had moved her kittens to the safety of the main house, where they now slept in the comfort of a drawer pulled from Jesse's bureau. Larry sighed and stuffed his weary body through the cat flap, its narrow sides scraping along his ribs. Need to quit with the extra slices of pizza, he brooded.

He padded into the office, then settled down on the pile of blankets under the desk, nose wrinkling at the powerful feline scent that Midnight's litter had left behind.

After resting his head on his paws and closing his eyes,

Larry's thoughts turned dark. He had messed up just about everything over the last few months ... or was it years? He admitted to himself with a sigh that it may have even been decades. Close to four centuries was a long time to spend as a Familiar, charged with protecting and aiding a varied succession of magical partners over many physical incarnations. Some of his magical partners had been very good at their jobs, others were not so good. A few had been downright awful at them.

For most of his very long life, he had always done his best. Paid attention. Kept his charges out of trouble. Protected them when needed. Loaned them his powerful magic. He'd been a good magical partner most of the time, he thought. Until the last fifty years or so.

The centuries-long grind had finally gotten to him. Mabel had been his magical partner for more than a hundred years. She had been one of the better ones—too good, in fact. His powerful witch partner had been so competent that she hadn't really needed much magical, administrative, or technical support from him. In fact, she had been so good that his skills and instincts had gone stale from disuse. He had gotten complacent, merely coasting through the motions instead of maintaining vigilance and honing his magic.

Despite what his friends said, Larry still felt that his inattention had contributed to Mabel's murder. Just because people were frighteningly competent didn't mean they couldn't use a hand now and then. Couldn't misjudge a situation. He had known something was wrong for months, but Mabel had assured him she could handle it—and she almost always could, so he had ignored his gut feelings and stood down. Then someone murdered Mabel. And those in the coven that he and Jesse trusted had betrayed them.

After that last awful coven meeting, with Litha gloating and the corrupt Councilman Jenkins backing her up, he and Jesse had been cast out and sent to a magical backwater, on a fool's errand, to protect an almost derelict supernatural scrapyard. Unbeknownst to them, of course, their new sleepy scrapyard home hid a galaxy-destroying magical machine within its rusting piles of metal waste.

Well, shit.

21

MOVING FORWARD

Larry's long night, followed by his early morning brooding, had left him exhausted. He quickly fell asleep on the blankets lining the abandoned kitten nursery. Nose twitching and legs bicycling in his sleep, he dreamed of many things. Running in wet grass, the sun warm on his fur. Laughing at jokes and japes shared with his friends. Working side by side with some of the greatest magical partners a Familiar could wish for. Really good pizza ...

Hours later, he woke with a start when a shaft of bright sunlight warmed his fur. Squinting blearily, Larry sat up and gazed around the room, soon realizing the sunlight heating his back end was streaming through a gap in the wooden boards hastily nailed over the shattered office window after the previous night's attack.

He shook his head to clear away the last remnants of his too vivid dreams. Stomach growling, Larry squeezed himself back through the cat flap, deciding it was high time to search out a late lunch ... or two.

As he picked his way gingerly across the forecourt, tying to avoid the small pieces of debris still littering the ground, Larry thanked Artemis, the goddess of Familiars, for his creation. So far, his life had been ... and was still good. Excellent, in fact. He just needed to recommit to living it again, instead of merely going through the motions ... to remember to trust his gut, be proactive—and make damn sure always to be there for his magical partner, whether or not they wanted his support.

AFTER A LATE LUNCH (OR TWO), an intense, multi-hour strategy session, and an early dinner, Larry found himself seated in the back seat of an ancient compact car heading north. After what felt like forever, he stretched his cramped muscles as street-lights whizzed by the car window. "Are we there, yet?" He whined.

Jesse, who was driving, glanced in the rear-view mirror and gave Larry the hairy eyeball. "No, we're not there yet, as you very well know, fur-face. You saw the Welcome to Boston signs we just passed as well as I did. It'll be another forty minutes until we reach Salem and arrive at our old covenstead." She turned her attention back to the highway with a huff of annoy-ance. "Who knew you'd be such a terrible traveler?"

Larry sneezed wetly, intentionally depositing a liberal coating of spit on the car's side window. He pushed his wet nose against the window and smeared it further. "I was just asking. Must have missed the highway signs. Besides, who says I can read?"

"Oh, knock it off dog-breath. I know darn well you can read —probably better than I can. After all, you've had more than a few centuries to learn." Jesse chuckled at her own comeback.

Cerri, who occupied the passenger seat of the small vehicle, stared absently out of the window at the dark scenery. "Will you two stop bickering? It's breaking my concentration. I need to make sure we aren't being followed, and my Earth magic doesn't work as well from a moving vehicle. Plus, you two are driving me crazy."

Larry met Jesse's eyes in the rearview mirror, and they exchanged a mutual grin. In unison, they chorused, "Sorry, Cerri!"

When Larry turned back to look out the window, he realized he'd smeared it so badly he couldn't see a thing. Grimacing in self-recrimination, he heaved his bulk across the seat to the still-clean window on the other side and gazed out at the darkness. He understood why they were making the hours' long drive to his old coven, instead of traveling by ley line—a trip of mere minutes, but he didn't have to like it.

When they discussed the trip to Salem during their strategy session that afternoon, Cerri had wisely pointed out it was likely the bad guys had a mage or two watching the area Crossroads to make sure no one left the scrapyard with the Universum and used the ley lines to escape. After the chaos of the previous night's battle, the mage watchers normally lurking outside the scrapyard's perimeter had withdrawn when the attackers retreated. But everyone agreed they would be back by tomorrow night.

During that morning's cleanup, Cerri's team had discovered several communications spells around the scrapyard perimeter, meaning their electronic devices were being monitored. The agents had deactivated the spells they found, but it was likely they hadn't discovered them all.

Larry knew that he and Jesse had only one way—and one night, to contact their old coven and request their help. They couldn't call. They couldn't email. They couldn't travel by ley line, so here they were ... on the road. In a tiny car. For hours. *Sigh.*

～

Earlier that evening, the trio had slipped through the scrapyard's back gate as twilight descended, then hurried to a rusty, paint-bleached old Honda Civic parked inconspicuously on a side street. The car belonged to the teenaged son of Ed the Beaver's witch partner. Ed had helped the kid out of a couple of scrapes with the traffic cops since he'd gotten his license, so he was happy to repay the favor, no questions asked.

Larry had heard the teen's muttered words to the beaver before the kid sloped away into the gathering darkness. "Just tell 'em not to wreck the car, Ed, or the old man'll kill me."

"Don't worry, everything will be okay," Ed had assured the worried teen. "Don't I always come through for you?"

As he watched the miles fly by, Larry just hoped Ed's optimism was warranted.

The vehicle's passengers lapsed into an uneasy silence during the last few miles to their destination. Wrapped in their own thoughts, each knew that much depended on the outcome of their upcoming meeting with Jesse and Larry's old coven mates.

Earlier that afternoon, Larry had used his surprisingly still-active mind link with the coven's Familiars to contact his raven friend. Sid had filled Larry in on coven happenings since he and Jesse had been exiled. The raven had explained that, immediately after the two departed for their new assignment at the scrapyard, Litha had conducted a leadership purge, then installed loyal cronies in all the top administrative positions. She had also banned all social gatherings not approved in advance by her newly appointed staff.

Sid had snickered when he shared the next bit of news. "What that bitch witch neglected to consider was how the demoted witches—and the rest of the disenfranchised coven members, would react to her coven takeover."

According to Sid, an underground network had quickly formed amongst the disaffected coven members. Since non-approved social gatherings of two or more witches were banned, their discontented Familiars facilitated communication amongst the would-be rebels via mind-speak and clandestine meetings in the woods. The best news was that the members of the resistance had done a lot of self-reflection since Litha took over, realizing they had become too complacent over the past several years. They all agreed that they had not paid enough attention to the dark political undercurrents that had begun when Litha and her friends joined the coven.

"To a witch, they've admitted not heeding their gut feelings about the way things were going in the coven, nor sharing their concerns with their High Priestess," Sid told Larry, smug satisfaction in his tone. "I'm quite proud of myself, though. I didn't tell them 'I told you so' more than, oh, half a dozen times."

Larry snickered at Sid's pleasure in being proven right about Litha, but couldn't help brooding about everything that had happened in the coven since Mabel's death.

He reflected bitterly that no coven members or Familiars had communicated their concerns to him either. Both he and Jesse had been Mabel's right-hand staff; anyone with concerns about suspicious goings on in the coven or amongst its members should have come to them first, before bothering Mabel. And when it was too late—when Mabel was dead and her killer was in the middle of a surprise takeover, no one had listened when he and Jesse raised the alarm. No one except Sid had stood up for them in the coven meeting, either.

Maybe he and Jesse weren't completely to blame for everything that had happened, Larry admitted to himself. Perhaps there had been more complacency and willful blindness infecting the coven than his and Jesse's, alone.

∾

JUST BEFORE MIDNIGHT, Jesse blew out an anxious breath and turned onto the narrow road leading to their old covenstead. The ancient oaks lining either side of the lane stretched heavy branches overhead, while dappled moonlight reflected on the car windows.

A massive midnight-black bird landed smoothly on the hood of their car just as they pulled to a stop in front of the covenstead. The raven peered through the windshield, an inquisitive tilt to his head. "Hey, Larry. Jesse. Long time no see."

"Hey, Sid. Same." Larry replied.

Jesse mumbled a greeting as she climbed out of the compact car. She opened the rear door for Larry, who hopped out, then stretched gratefully, before padding into a patch of moonlight glinting on the gravel drive.

The raven flapped his wings briefly before gliding to the ground next to his canine friend. Glinting in the moonlight, a small piece of metal half-buried under the driveway's gravel and dirt surface caught the massive bird's eye. He expertly clawed at the ground, exposing a metal pull tab from a long-empty soda can. "Cool, a 1980s Dr. Pepper tab. Don't have one of these in my collection," the raven croaked delightedly.

Larry suppressed a snort of impatience and nervously eyed the covenstead, hoping their arrival had not been noted while Sid cawed over his discovery. Sid was a raven, after all; he just could not resist shiny things—although it was news to Larry that the acquisitive bird had what sounded like an extensive soda tab collection.

Seeking to redirect the raven's attention to the reason for their presence, Larry asked, "So, what's the scoop, Sid?"

The raven tore his gaze from his shiny new acquisition, cocked his head, and fixed Larry with a beady eye. "There's no need to worry about Litha's crew, bud. After you and me mind-spoke this afternoon, those of us not aligned with Litha and her cronies realized we needed to get off our collective duffs and take back the coven. We've got Litha's lapdogs locked up in the null-magic cells under the covenstead. Those traitors can cool their heels there while we sort this mess out, then we'll hand them—and that bitch Litha, if she ever shows back up, over to the Witch Council for punishment."

With a quick twist of his head, Sid fixed Jesse with an apologetic eye. "Uh, Jesse. Just wanted to say sorry for what happened before. Our bad."

"No worries, Sid." Jesse's soft smile contrasted with the sadness in her eyes. "We all messed this one up, didn't we?"

Cerri, who had remained silent while the old friends exchanged greetings, pointedly cleared her throat, reminding Larry of their current mission. "Sid, this is Cerri, Earth witch and Priestess of Cerridwen. She's the SBI agent whose team is hunting the jacka ... idiots who are bent on ending life as we know it."

Sid eyed Cerri for a moment, then head his dipped in respectful acknowledgement. "Hail and Welcome, Priestess of Cerridwen. I, and the rest of my coven—those not in the dungeon, anyway—are at your service. Perhaps we should all head inside so you can bring us up to date."

The trio followed Sid as he flew towards the covenstead. As they stepped onto the porch, a set of beautifully carved double doors swung open wide, welcoming light spilling out from within. Half a dozen relieved witches filled the doorway, with more behind, all of them chattering at once.

"Welcome home, Jesse."

"Hey, Larry."

"We are soooo sorry, guys."

"We should have listened to you."

"We gave those assholes what for, though."

"Hope they like their crappy cells."

Overwhelmed, Larry and Jesse hung back, but Cerri placed a firm hand on each of their backs and pushed them towards the open door, whispering encouragement. "Come on, you two. Time to stop looking back and move forward."

In a louder voice, Cerri addressed the gathered witches and Familiars. "Let's move this meeting inside, everyone. We have a lot to discuss, and not a lot of time to do it."

THE RETURN TRIP to the scrapyard would be much faster, as almost everyone would travel by ley line. There was really no way to hide the arrival of a covenful of witches, along with their Familiars, so they had decided not to try. Besides, with so many magical reinforcements, the scrapyard defenders would soon be ready to implement the next part of their plan.

Before they left, Cerri had called in a few favors from agents at the Boston SBI office. Within the hour, half a dozen black-suited mages had arrived and taken custody of Litha's unhappy co-conspirators.

Larry snickered at the dark sunglasses the SBI agents sported—even though it was well after midnight and dark as pitch outside. Talk about imitation being the sincerest form of flattery. These guys must have watched *Men in Black* waaayyy too many times, he mused.

Cerri discreetly nudged him and mind-spoke a rebuke. *"You're just jealous. You only wish you could carry off that G-Man look."*

Larry's only response to Cerri's teasing was a discreet side-eye, although he assured himself silently, *"Nah, I'm happy with my junkyard dog look. Thank you very much."*

Cerri hid a smile, but Jesse's snicker informed Larry that he wasn't very good at hiding his thoughts. Not that he should hide them from his magical partner, he admitted, especially considering his new commitment to trust and communication.

"FOLLOW ME, EVERYONE," Cerri instructed as she headed toward the Crossroads. "It's time to get to work saving the galaxy."

Several dozen witches cackled in delight and followed the SBI agent down the driveway, accompanied by their equally excited Familiars.

Larry followed the crowd towards the Crossroads, but not before throwing a worried glance back at the ancient Honda still parked in front of the covenstead, and at the even more ancient witch standing beside it, keys clutched in her arthritic hands.

The elderly witch would drive Ed's teenage friend's car back to the scrapyard, hopefully arriving just before dawn. Larry had insisted they honor their promise to get the kid's car back to him. He just hoped the crone could see well enough behind her thick glasses to get the damn thing there in one piece.

22

KITTEN CONTINGENCIES

The arrival of more than a dozen extra witches, along with their Familiars, taxed the admittedly limited accommodations at the scrapyard. However, most of the newcomers had been settled on a bed, couch, or air mattress in either the main house or the office by the wee hours of the morning.

Larry, curled nose to tail at the bottom of Jesse's bed, napped fitfully, but was awake by the time the golden light of the new day reached his position on the comfortable mattress. He knew they had little time to organize and execute their strategy to defend the scrapyard long enough to unearth the Universum and spirit it far away to a new hiding place. Hopefully, their plans would be successful. Not that anyone would be around to worry about it if they weren't. Failure would mean no more Earth. No more Milky Way. No more supernatural realms. No more anything.

At the sounds of activity coming from the kitchen, Larry shook off his dark thoughts, jumped off the bed, and hurried downstairs. If this was going to be his last day here ... well, anywhere, he was not willing to miss enjoying a hearty breakfast ... or two.

By late morning, everyone was awake, if not rested. The new arrivals took shifts patrolling the scrapyard, adding an extra layer of security in readiness for the inevitable battle to come. The mobster's mage watchers had returned to their posts outside the perimeter just before dawn, and they were no longer bothering to hide their presence or mask their dark intentions.

Fortunately, everyone agreed that Michael and his co-conspirators were unlikely to attack in force during daylight hours, so they had until darkness fell that evening to organize the scrapyard's defense ... and free the hostages, and find the Universum, and get the damn thing far away—before the bad guys got their hands on it. *Piece of cake. Not.*

THEY FILLED the daylight hours with planning and preparation for the battle to come. The newly enlarged team of defenders eagerly undertook their work, which included strengthening the wards and constructing defenses, both magical and mundane, around the scrapyard.

Just after lunch, Cerri's SBI team, along with Jesse and several of her former coven mates, plus Larry, Midnight, and Carb, sequestered themselves in the office for several intense hours of strategizing. Shafts of multicolored sunlight streamed into the room from the newly repaired windows above the desk. One of Larry's former coven members had a magical affinity with glass. It had taken her mere moments, as well as a handful of dirt scooped from the large flowerpot by the office door, to repair the shattered glass. She had even shown off her magical skills by adding a stained glass insert at the top of each window.

Cerri stood near the desk, purple and blue light from the stained glass dappling her long red hair and highlighting her attractive face. After the botched rescue attempt at the old marina, she and the rest of her team had not resumed their old lady disguises. The bad guys now knew Cerri and the rest of her SBI agents were involved in the scrapyard's defense, so there was no point. Besides, it would be easier to fight in leathers than in velour tracksuits and voluminous house-dresses. Jesse had grumbled about how damn comfortable her sweatpants were, but smiled in reluctant delight when Cerri produced a set of leathers in just her size.

"Okay guys, listen up. Here's the plan." Cerri's raised voice quieted the room's chatter. "I've contacted the local SBI office apprised them of the situation. They are going to liaise with their counterparts in the FBI. They'll have several teams in place outside the scrapyard by nightfall —"

Jesse interrupted Cerri, confusion and worry writ large in her expression. "The FBI? Is it wise to involve a mundane law enforcement agency in supernatural matters?"

Cerri's wise eyes sparkled with suppressed mirth. "Do you really think mundane law enforcement, especially at the highest levels, isn't aware of the supernatural? While the SBI is excellent at policing supernatural matters, we can't be every-where. Over the years, we have developed relationships with most major mundane law enforcement agencies around the world. In fact, the FBI team arriving tonight has more mages and witches on it than humans."

"Shows what I know," Jesse murmured, eyes wide in surprise. "Sorry I interrupted, Cerri."

"No problem, Jesse. It was a legitimate question. I'm sure several of your former coven mates present for this meeting were wondering the same thing."

"Yeah, my former coven mates..." Jesse murmured, her eyes flicking around the room, seeking the faces of her former friends. She dropped her gaze, grief clouding her expression. Larry pressed himself against his magical partner's knee, offering comfort. A ghost of a smile curved Jesse's lips, and she stretched a hand down to scratch behind his ear.

"Oh goddess, that feels good! Thanks Jess!" Larry mind-spoke as his back leg moved in unison with Jesse's hand. Face brightening at her Familiar's antics, Jesse straightened her shoulders and sat up, determined to stop letting past traumas cloud her present.

Cerri cleared her throat and resumed her report, but not before adding a cryptic remark. "We'll see about that 'former' part. Here's the deal, everyone. The FBI agents that will be stationed outside the perimeter tonight can't actively assist with the magical end of things, since the SBI will oversee tonight's operation because most of the major players are supes, however they can help with arresting the bad guys once they break mundane law." Grimly, she added. "It's not legal to fire-bomb buildings or shoot at people, whether using mundane or magical means."

"How can you be sure the bad guys are going to attack the scrapyard tonight?" Carb asked curiously. The little demon perched on the desk, idly fishing out metal paperclips from a magnetic holder and munching on them.

"Because we are going to make them," Cerri replied, her sharp eyes glittering with gleeful anticipation.

After a moment of stunned silence, everyone started talking at once.

"What?!"

"How are we going to do that?"

"Why would we do that?"

Cerri patted the air and asked for quiet. Finally, when the hubbub showed no sign of slowing, she shouted. "SILENCE!!!" The powerful Earth witch had put some magical oomph into her command—enough to rattle the floorboards and shake the newly repaired windows, which scattered multicolored drops of sunlight across the faces of those present.

When a shocked silence reined, Cerri merely nodded and began again. "Let me explain how things will go down tonight." No one interrupted the SBI team leader after that, and most everyone agreed her plan was brilliant. It would work. It had to.

CERRI EXPLAINED she had sent Sid on an errand earlier that day. The enormous bird had soared off with two messages clasped in his beak. The first was addressed to Michael Malfisco, the magical mobster after the Universum, while the second was addressed to the very corrupt Councilman Jenkins, who, while ostensibly working in partnership with the mobster, almost certainly had his own dark plans for the device.

Both of Cerri's messages offered each man the same thing: the Universum in exchange for the hostages. The two men would have to work together if they wanted a chance to get their hands on the deadly device. Cerri had issued a deadline for her offer: they must bring the hostages to the scrapyard by nightfall that evening for the handover. And Ted and Risa must be alive, or all bets were off.

Larry realized that Cerri's idea to send separate messages was actually brilliant. The two men would have to continue working together, at least at first. Larry had no illusions about the friable partnership between the mobster and the corrupt councilman but the dueling messages would ensure both men brought their full contingent of magic users, since each side almost certainly planned to double-cross the other once they had possession of the Universum.

When Midnight expressed concern for the safety of Ted, her magical partner, and one of the two hostages, Cerri reassured her. "It's best if we have the hostages brought to us, so we have the home court advantage for their rescue. I'm sure that Michael and the councilman will come prepared to do battle tonight—first with us, and then with each other. After all, we've given them the perfect opportunity. They each want the Universum and will assume we won't fight back during the exchange for fear of injuring the hostages and the deal falling through."

Carb's gravelly words dripped with horrified disbelief. "So, we get them to bring their full teams, all ready for battle, along with the hostages ... and we just hand over the Universum? Then what?"

Larry glanced around the room. Cerri's team wore battle-hardened expressions, which told him there was more to Cerri's scheme than Carb thought. "So, what's the scoop, Cerri? How do we free the hostages, hang on to the Universum, and defeat the bad guys once and for all?"

"Oh, they'll do most of that all by themselves, Familiar," Cerri replied.

The wily SBI agent's malevolent grin unsettled Larry. "Huh? But how?" He asked, confused and not a little terrified by the frighteningly cunning woman before him.

"We'll do it with a little help from our friends, of course. That's why Carb is here."

Cerri gestured at the little demon, who looked up from his paper clip snacking, eyes wide.

Carb in confusion. "I thought I was here to give an update on finding the Universum."

"You'll do that, too, Carb," Cerri replied. "But mainly, you are here as the representative of your fellow ferrous demons. We'll need your help if we're going to pull tonight's plan off." She grimaced and added, "It's a good plan, but there are a lot of moving parts to it—and you and your demon friends have a large part to play to ensure its success."

Carb gave a bemused shrug. "Okaaaayyy. How can we help?"

"You guys love to eat metal, right?" Cerri asked, grinning down at the little demon.

"Well, duh. Of course, we do. Ferrous demons here, remember?" Carb's confusion increased, along with his sarcasm.

"I seriously doubt the bad guys are going to walk here, Carb," Cerri explained with a sly smile. "They'll travel here in cars, vans, maybe even a minibus or two ... so there will be lots and lots of nice, fresh metal for you all to snack on." She leaned forward and fixed the now-nervous Carb with an intent gaze. "You are ferrous demons, my friend; the bad guys can't easily kill your kind. Fire doesn't affect you, projectiles will bounce off your tough hides, and bullets are merely for snacking on. Am I right?"

"Well, yeeessss," Carb drawled reluctantly. "Although we prefer to eat in peace, in the shadows ... not in the middle of a magical battle. Catching bullets in mid-air sounds like a lot of work. Not that we couldn't do it, mind you. We're fast. Like really, really fast, and—"

Larry interrupted Carb's monologue, his voice filled with hope and excitement. "I think I see where Cerri's going with this, Carb! While we're negotiating with the bad guys, you and your demon buddies can make your way to the van holding the hostages. Once the bad guys attack us—and they will—your job will be to munch your way through the bottom of the van and free them."

He swiveled his gaze to his new favorite SBI mastermind and confirmed, "That's part of the plan. Right, Cerri? We'll definitely need a big distraction so the demons can do their thing ...."

Cerri grinned smugly. "Powerful Earth witch and Priestess of Cerridwen here, remember? I'll create an earthquake or two and maybe a rainstorm as diversions so the demons can free the hostages and get them away from the battlefield via the tunnels before things get too intense." She flicked a sharp gaze around the room. "Once the demons free Ted and Risa, we'll counterattack. Our augmented forces here in the scrapyard are now a match for theirs. Plus, we'll have backup outside the gates: the local SBI and FBI teams will move in from the rear."

"That's definitely a bunch of moving parts, guys. Lots could go wrong." Jesse's doubt tempered the excitement simmering in the room.

"We'll pull it off, Jesse. We have no choice." Larry's simple statement fell into the room like a stone, sending ripples of determination outward until they touched everyone present. They really had no choice but to win.

AFTER THAT, there wasn't much more to say, so the meeting ended, and the energized plotters filed out of the office, chattering about the coming showdown. Larry followed Carb towards the door, but a soft feline voice delayed his exit.

"Larry, wait. I need a word with you," Midnight whispered as she peered intently down at him from her perch on top of a filing cabinet. She flicked a glance at Carb and gestured with her chin. Obviously, this was to be a private conversation.

Carb merely shrugged and loped after the others, while Larry turned back and hopped up onto the desk, not wanting to strain his neck during his chat with the enigmatic cat. "What's up, Midnight?"

The small black cat gazed at him, her green eyes serious and sad. "You know I'm going to have to leave tonight with Ted, right? Once the demons free Ted, the plan is for us to slip away with the Universum during the chaos of the battle." She sighed deeply, resignation and regret settling on her feline features.

"My job as the Felinus Universum doesn't end tonight, Larry. In fact, as long as I'm alive, it will never end."

"Wait, what?" Larry sputtered. "But what about your kittens? They're too young to hit the road with you — oh. Oh, no. No, you don't. You can't leave me in charge of your little furlings. I'm not cat-dad material. I'm not anybody's dad material." Larry's ears flapped wildly as he shook his head in vigorous denial.

Midnight purred a laugh. "I'm not asking you to adopt my kittens, numb-nuts. But I need someone I trust to make sure they're safe and get them where they need to go once the battle is over. I'm sure DEAF already has their first assignments lined up. The kits are old enough now to bond with their new magical partners, who can give them the care and training they need as they grow up."

Not done with his objections, Larry growled, "But I'm going to be very busy during the battle. I'll have ... shit to do!"

Midnight rolled her eyes at his vociferous protestations. "Of course you'll have shit to do during the fight, you dingleberry. Everyone will. But I need to know someone I trust will look out for the kits and get them away from here afterwards ...." Midnight paused and shrugged in resignation. "Well, if there is an afterwards, that is."

Larry snapped his muzzle shut and lowered his ears in defeat. Midnight trusted him. She had said so, more than once. Considering his new commitment to mutual trust and to proactively helping those closest to him, how could he say no? "Alright, cat. Let's tuck your kittens somewhere safe for now, then I'll ensure they get to their new homes once things settle down."

Midnight purred loudly, then jumped expertly off the cabinet onto the desk. She rubbed her face against Larry's in unspoken thanks.

Larry and Midnight worked together to move the kittens

from Jesse's bedroom into the windowless basement, where the little kittens soon slept snuggled up on a pile of blankets wedged behind the water heater.

Midnight gave Larry a feral smile. "I have placed strong protective wards around the basement. Nothing and no one can get in here. They'll die trying, first."

Larry's muzzle gaped in shock. "Hopefully, the wards won't affect me. How am I going to foster these fur-balls if I can't get to 'em ... or die trying?"

"Of course, the wards won't affect you, idiot. Only those with ill intent." Midnight's narrowed eyes questioned Larry's intelligence and the wisdom of her decision to trust him with her progeny. She sighed and shook her head. "Luckily, brains aren't required for what I need you to do."

"Right. Of course." Larry ignored the grieving mama-cat's insults and backed off. "The wards won't affect me. Silly me for thinking they would."

After Larry's uncomfortable ascendence to feline foster-dad, he padded up the steep basement steps and headed outside, leaving Midnight to bid a teary farewell to her brood. He rolled his neck as he went. Hoooo boy. Talk about straining his commitment to trusting his gut and taking responsibility for protecting those in his circle.

Did you have to test me so soon, Artemis? Larry threw his rhetorical question to the skies. He could swear he heard faint feminine laughter floating on the midafternoon breeze.

IT TOOK A GOOD HALF HOUR, but Larry finally corralled Carb for a private chat. The two huddled in one of the tunnels dug by Carb's industrious team of demons while on the hunt for the Universum. Larry listened intently, then sent his magic out to search the length of the tunnel. They were alone. Good.

"Carb, I've got kind of a big favor to ask," Larry whispered. He paused and fixed Carb with worried eyes.

"Spit it out, bud. What's up?" Carb replied patiently. The little demon sat cross-legged on the fresh earth of the tunnel, absently picking at a small piece of metal embedded in the ground near his feet. "I'm all ears."

Larry heaved a sigh and sat, heedless of the muddy surface under his rear. He knew his next words would reinforce his commitment to trust his gut ... and that of those around him. It would also cement his determination to protect those close to him from now on. "I, uh ... I may need your help. After the battle."

The pair sat in amiable silence for a while as Larry wrestled with voicing his request.

Carb finally interrupted Larry's pained musings and asked, "Well? What do you need me to do?"

Larry reluctantly responded. "You probably know by now that Midnight is leaving me in charge of her kittens. She has to leave with Ted and the Universum tonight, during the battle. It's her job to protect that blasted thing, and she won't abandon her responsibilities." He sighed and got to the point. "But she can't take the kittens on the road, so...."

"Yes. I knowwww." Carb drew out his words. "But what does that have to do with me?"

"Well, here's the thing. I've got a bad feeling about tonight. Oh, I think we'll succeed in freeing the hostages and getting the Universum safely away from here, but ... dammit, I'm just not sure." Larry shook his head and growled in frustration. "My gut is telling me I need to make contingency plans for the kittens."

The little demon's enormous eyes widened. "Oh, no. Nope, not taking on kitten duties. Not even for you, Larry."

Larry patted the air with his paw. "I'm not asking you to, Carb. I've got it. Unless I ... don't." Larry paused, his intense gaze seeking his friend's worried one. "It's just ... if anything happens to me, I need you to get the kittens away from here. Take them to the Furry Friends animal shelter in Westport. It's just a couple towns over. That's where DEAF has arranged for the kits' magical partners to find them. Can you do that for me, please? Obviously, only if I ... uh, can't, for some reason."

Carb growled, his face a mask of pain and anger. "Don't you say that, Larry. We ... you will survive this battle. You can damn well take the kittens there yourself, once this is all over."

"But if I can't, Carb," Larry insisted. "I just have a feeling ... promise me you'll see the kittens get to the shelter?" Larry's body tensed. This was hard, asking for help. Trusting his gut. Trusting others. Fuck. Larry sent another silent message to the goddess of Familiars. *I hope you appreciate my self-improvement efforts, Artemis.*

Carb's long fingers closed around Larry's paw and gently squeezed it. "I'll do it, Larry. I promise. I'll make sure the kittens get their furry asses dumped at that shelter, no matter what."

The two friends sat in silence for a moment, then Larry snickered. "Furry asses, huh?"

"Well, their asses *are* furry." Carb's honest answer sent Larry over the edge. He barked in laughter, then couldn't stop.

Carb joined him, his rough, grumbly chuckles echoing off the tunnel's earthen walls.

After a while, mirth spent, Larry stood and shook the dirt off his fur. "I'm starving; let's go see what's for dinner. I'm sure we can rustle you up a nice plate of metal, but I'm gonna have a slice or three of that pot-roast I smelled cooking earlier."

The friends ambled out of the tunnel into the late afternoon sunshine.

23

CADILLAC CATASTROPHE

O nce she had extracted the promise from Larry to care for her kittens after she left, Midnight had sequestered herself with the ferrous demons guarding the location of the Universum. While she had needed to call on all her skills as the Felinus Universum and work powerful but intricate magic, by late afternoon, Midnight had successfully deactivated the Universum's wards and prepared the deadly machine for transport.

Cerri's team had been busy most of the afternoon, planting dangerous magical surprises around the scrapyard's perimeter. Jesse's former coven mates spent the afternoon reinforcing the wards and preparing defensive battle spells. One elderly witch was heard to comment that she hadn't had so much fun since the war. No one wanted to incur the crone's wrath by asking exactly which war. Considering her advanced age, it could have been anything from the Revolutionary War onwards.

As the sun dipped behind the trees, the local Familiars, led by Ed the Beaver, disguised themselves as mundane animals and slunk out of the scrapyard, before strategically positioning themselves in trees and shrubs around the area. The Familiars from Larry and Jesse's former coven remained in the scrapyard; their job was to provide magical power to their witch partners during the coming battle.

At Carb's request, the demons not on Universum guard duty had outdone themselves. Ferrous demons excelled at tunneling. It was a survival skill their species had mastered during their long existence in the Underworld, where traveling amongst the dangerous creatures inhabiting that realm's surface was too dangerous for such small, magically weak demons.

Their expertise at tunneling had saved Carb's species from extinction once—and needed to do so again. An elaborate tunnel system now honeycombed the area around the front and back gates, both inside the perimeter fence and extending well beyond it. The demons should be able to approach the van carrying the hostages, sight unseen.

By the time the sun slipped below the horizon, the scrapyard defenders were in place and awaiting their enemies—and the hostages. An owl hooted in the growing dusk, then another responded with a matching cry, informing the defenders that their enemies were approaching. Larry and Jesse stood in the front line, along with Cerri and her SBI team.

Cerri had objected to their presence, wanting them to be in the scrapyard's second line of defense, but one look at their stubborn faces had told her the pair would not budge.

"This scrapyard is our assignment Tant, whether or not we wanted it to be. We're not gonna let you lot do all the defending of it," Jesse insisted, her jaw jutting pugnaciously. Larry's lips curled in a snarl of agreement.

"Alright, you two. Just ... be ready. And follow my team's lead." Cerri's narrowed eyes drilled home her command.

"Yes, ma'am." Larry touched his paw to his forehead in a salute.

Jesse snickered and gave Cerri a sloppy salute of her own.

"I'm done with you two. On your own heads be it." Cerri threw up her hands and marched away, shouting orders to her team as she did so.

BEFORE LONG, a caravan of cars, SUVs, and vans pulled into the road leading to the main gate. The driveway could not accommodate all the vehicles, so most pulled up in the weeds on either side of the paved drive. Larry's Familiar sources stationed outside the fence-line informed him that another half dozen vehicles had arrived and now blocked the back gate, as well.

What was obviously the lead vehicle, a shiny, black Cadillac with darkly tinted windows, pulled to a smooth stop ten yards from the front gate. Several large SUVs pulled up behind and to each side, obviously intent on protecting the VIPs inside the Cadillac.

After a tense moment, the Cadillac's front doors opened, and the vehicle lurched as its occupants disembarked. Larry recognized Michael Malfisco and Councilman Jenkins as they alighted from the vehicle. The councilman quickly distanced himself from his partner in crime, striding over to one of the SUVs as his men exited the large vehicle and surrounded him protectively.

Larry snickered at the posturing between the two rivals, but his amusement was cut short when two other figures emerged from the Cadillac's rear doors. Well, fuck.

Carlos Giotti rose to his full height, casually brushing the creases out of his expensive Italian suit. His tanned face, all angles and wrinkles, turned towards the gate, a wintery smile stretching his thin lips. Beside Carlos stood his only other surviving grandson, Anthony Manucci.

Carlos spread his hands and growled, "That's right, ladies and gentlemen; I'm in charge of this shindig." The hard-faced mobster chuckled and waved a disparaging hand at his grandsons. "Did you really think these two fools ... or indeed any of my useless progeny, could have come up with a plan like this on their own?"

Michael's lips thinned, while Anthony's face darkened. But neither responded to their grandfather's insults. It was apparent that Carlos controlled his biological family with the same cruel iron fist he did his criminal one.

The crime boss strode forward toward and faced the scrapyard's defenders, his face a mask of hate. As he studied the scrapyard defenders, two massively muscled bodyguards strode protectively to his side, hands inside their suit jackets, obviously resting on their guns.

Somehow, Carlos discerned Cerri was in charge, because he fixed her with a contemptuous glare and snorted. "I see they've put a woman in charge of this failed enterprise ... how like the SBI."

He shook his head and grinned gleefully. "That'll just make things easier for me. Anyway, before we start, I want to reiterate that I've been pulling the strings on this operation from behind the scenes from the very beginning. I'm fully aware that both the SBI and the FBI are currently investigating my organization. Both agencies have been after me for years, of course. But this time, they have had some inside help, and their joint investigations have come rather too close for comfort."

Carlos flicked an enigmatic glance at his stoic grandsons and smiled slyly. "It's time for me to hit the road — or rather, the skies. With the help of the Universum, I plan to build a criminal enterprise that's truly out of this world ... or is it galaxy?" He chuckled merrily at his own joke, then snapped an order to the burly men at his side. "Take care of my grandsons."

The senior mobster's bodyguards quickly approached the two men, guns raised. Eyes wide and confused, Carlos's grandsons tentatively raised their hands, peering in growing fear at their grandfather, who sneered at their shocked faces. "Do you think I don't know you two idiots have been feeding the cops information about my organization? Once you got rid of the rest of your sniveling competition, you fools teamed up to take me out, didn't you? And what better way to put me out of commission than to have me locked up for twenty-five to life in a mundane prison ... or sentenced to death by the Supernatural Council?"

"You cowards!" Carlos spat. Face twisted in a rictus of hatred, he glared at his terror-stricken grandsons. "Why couldn't either of you face me like men? Instead, you had to run to the cops, squealing like the rats you are." The mobster nodded once, face impassive as he passed judgement on his petrified grandchildren. Flicking a glance at his bodyguards, he snarled, "Shoot 'em both."

Gunshots rang out in the night air and both men dropped to the ground, growing pools of blood expanding under their still bodies.

Face impassive, Carlos studied the dead men and shook his head. "Fools," he muttered, before turning his hard gaze on the shocked defenders gathered inside the scrapyard fence, a cruel smile on his lips. He gestured at the fallen men. "You see what I'm willing to do to my own flesh and blood who have betrayed and defied me. Imagine what I'll do to you? Hand over the Universum and I'll leave. Peacefully."

The rich, iron smell of blood tainted the night air, belying the mobster's promise. Everyone present knew that no one was getting out of this peacefully. And many would not see the dawn.

Cerri slipped through the gate and closed it securely behind her. After casting a fleeting glance at the dead men, she strode over to Carlos. Meeting his glare head-on, she calmly said, "First, you show us the hostages. We need proof of life before this deal goes any further."

Carlos chuckled, his gaze flicking to a white panel van bearing a plumber's logo that was parked in the weeds twenty yards away. "The hostages are present. But you'll have to take my word for it, I'm afraid. First, hand over the Universum, witch."

"No," Carrie stated firmly.

"No?" Carlos raised one eyebrow in amused query.

"Fuck, no, asshole," Cerri replied, an amused smile curving her lips. She widened her stance and planted her hands firmly on her hips. "Is that better, old man?"

Larry snorted in laughter at Cerri's brave words. "Boy, that witch has brass — um. Yeah, those," he muttered to Jesse, who snickered and nodded her agreement.

Carlos's face puckered in anger, and he barked an order at his men. "Grab her!"

As his subordinates hurried to obey, Cerri quickly pulled several small vials from her pockets and threw them on the ground. Then all hell broke loose. The ground shook violently and crevices appeared, quickly widening as they branched out in every direction. Amidst shouts of awe and terror, Cerridwen's priestess screamed her goddess's name at the night sky and the heavens opened, rain pelting down as the wind whipped up, great gusts driving the rain sideways.

Carlos swore and hurried back to his car; his shoulders hunched against the tempest. Just before ducking inside his sleek vehicle, the mobster screamed a command. "Attack the scrapyard! Kill them all, if you have to, but get me that damned Universum!"

THE BATTLE that followed would go down in the annals of the SBI as one of the fiercest the agency ever fought. Magically, the opposing forces were almost evenly matched, which made the fight even more vicious and left the outcome in doubt until the very end. The mobster's mages rained gunfire and magic on those protecting the scrapyard, while the defenders matched their deadly attacks with those of their own.

From his vantage point just inside the gate, Larry's eyes swept the battle scene, haunches tensed as he decided where to attack. His eyes widened when he spotted a group of enemy mages join hands and start chanting, their gazes fixed on the fence surrounding the scrapyard.

A witch to Larry's right screamed a warning. "The wards are weakening! We can't hold them much longer."

Larry howled a war cry and raced toward the fence line, barking a command to the closest Familiars. "Help me, everyone! We've got to stop those mage chanters, or they'll crack the wards!"

He didn't wait to see if his fellow Familiars obeyed the command; he had to trust his team would respond to his call. Instead, he squeezed his large body through the same loose piece of fencing that he had used to help Midnight bring her kittens into the scrapyard just days ago and raced toward the chanting mages. A deafening crack rent the air before Larry could reach them and someone shouted, "They've broken the wards!" Screams of pain and terror echoed through the night as the fighting raged around him.

With the wards broken, Larry knew the battle to protect the scrapyard was lost. But they could still win the war—if the ferrous demons freed the hostages from the van in time. Then Ted and Midnight could spirit the Universum away from the fight and the galaxy would be safe. At least for now.

Leaving the magically spent enemy mages to the claws and teeth of his fellow Familiars, Larry dodged left and raced towards the white plumber's van he suspected contained the hostages. He had to distract the guards, giving the ferrous demons the time they needed to finish chewing their way through the bottom of the vehicle so they could free the hostages.

As he approached the van, he growled in horror at the scene before him. One mobster had a machine gun aimed at the van's windscreen, his finger tightening on the trigger, while another had his charged wand aimed at the vehicle's sliding doors.

Larry roared in anger and launched himself at the man with the gun. Just as his teeth ripped into the man's throat, a sharp pain numbed his back legs. Larry growled fiercely and held on, jaw grinding, until both he and his victim hit the ground. Then everything went black.

24

DOG OF THE HOUR

"Larry? Larry! Wake up, bud." Gentle hands gingerly stroked Larry's flank.

Jesse's entreaties and warm hands brought Larry slowly back to consciousness. Without moving his head, he opened his eyes and scanned the room. Lots of worried faces, both witch and Familiar, gazed back at him anxiously.

"Oh, shit. It's bad, isn't it?" Larry mind-spoke the question to Jesse. A strange numbness filled his core, but there was no pain, thankfully.

"Afraid so, sweetie." Sorrow laced Jesse's reply.

"I knew something was off about the whole scrapyard thing," Larry mumbled. "But did we win?"

Cerri sat gingerly on the edge of the bed. One side of her face was swollen and bruised, and she had one arm wrapped around what were no doubt several broken ribs. The SBI team leader and priestess of Cerridwen smiled at Larry, her eyes full of wisdom and pain. "Yes, Larry, we won — thanks to you. Your heroic actions gave the ferrous demons the time they needed to chew through the bottom of the van and rescue the hostages."

She smiled softly and confirmed Larry's fervent hope. "Ted and Midnight got the Universum away from the scrapyard safely. From what I understand, they've left the country in search of a new—and hopefully more secure, hiding place for their magical burden."

"Oh, that's great news," Larry murmured as he studied the SBI agent critically. "You look like you've been in the wars yourself, Cerri. That's quite a black eye you've got there. Several broken ribs, too, I suspect."

Cerri touched her face and chuckled, then grimaced in pain and wrapped her arm more tightly around her injured ribs. "This? I've had much worse, Larry."

A malicious grin curved the injured woman's lips. "Oh, and just so you know, the Boston SBI office arrested Litha early this morning. Agents found her trying to sneak into the ley line at a small Crossroads just outside of town. Turns out she heard about her co-conspirator's defeat and her coven's defection to the side of truth and justice and made a run for it. She'll stand trial for her part in this, along with the rest of her co-conspirators."

"And for Mabel's murder," Larry queried. "Will they charge her with Mabel's murder, too?"

Cerri's eyes twinkled, but something dark and deadly lurked behind her amusement. "Litha has already confessed to Mabel's murder, Larry."

She grinned fiercely. "Obviously, Litha would rather be handed over to the local police and be charged with a mundane murder than charged and sentenced by the SBI for her role in the Universum plot. We all know very well what that would mean for her. Thankfully, the SBI is retaining jurisdiction and the Supernatural Council has charged her with high treason."

Larry nodded mutely, knowing that supernatural justice was swift and harsh. Litha would soon suffer an unpleasant death for her part in the Universum plot. "What happened after I ... well, you know," he asked, rolling his eyes down to indicate his damaged body.

"The FBI took Carlos's non-magical henchmen into custody—the ones that survived, anyway. Councilman Jenkins and Carlos Giotti were both injured, but they'll live long enough to stand trial before the Supernatural Council." Cerri's gaze dropped as she finished her update. "I'm afraid Cleo got away, bud. But her criminal behavior has earned her an Order of Destruction. DEAF will catch up with her before long, I'm sure."

Larry heaved a satisfied sigh. "Karma's a bitch. If anyone deserves what DEAF will do to her, it's that damned cat." Exhausted, his eyes drifted closed, but reopened when the bed dipped with another passenger. He roused himself with effort and greeted the new arrival. "Risa! Great to see you. You good?"

The Water witch was pale and had dark circles under her eyes, but she smiled softly at Larry. "I'm good," she murmured as she gently stroked Larry's dirty, bloodstained head.

FOR SEVERAL LONG MINUTES, the room's air hung heavy with both great sadness and deep relief, and silence settled over the room's occupants.

Then Cerri straightened, adopted a businesslike manner, and met Larry's tired gaze. "Familiar, DEAF has informed me they have an important new assignment for you, so you'll soon be returning to the Underworld and heading back to the DEAF Headquarters. You know the drill: your caseworker will brief you on your new assignment and assign your new physical form. After that, DEAF will send you back to Earth to meet up with your new magical partner."

Cerri hesitated, her eyes filling with tears. She grinned crookedly, then leaned down and whispered into Larry's ear. "When we found you after the battle, I asked Hades to give us a few moments with you before you ... uh, left, so that we could thank you for your heroic efforts and ... say goodbye."

Larry's eyes widened in shock; this courageous woman had some serious supernatural pull if she could request a favor like that from the god of the Underworld—and have it granted. "Uh, okay. Thanks, Cerri ... I think." He flicked a glance at Jesse, who remained by his side, stroking him gently, her eyes filled with regret and resignation. "But who's gonna be Jesse's new Familiar? She can't manage this scrapyard on her own. Can't DEAF, you know, just give me a new body and send me back here?"

Cerri simply shook her head mutely, so Risa answered on her behalf. "The scrapyard was almost completely destroyed in the battle, Larry. The only magical item of real value, the Universum, is no longer here. Midnight's extra heavy-duty wards are the only reason the cottage is still standing. When she warded the basement to protect her kittens, she included the rest of the house, too, just to be on the safe side, I guess."

Picking up the explanation, Cerri said, "The Supernatural Council has given what remains of the property to the ferrous demons. They appointed Carb as scrapyard manager. Oh, and the house Brownie will go with Jesse when she leaves." She snickered and added, "Violet asked me to remind you of your promise. Her exact words were, *'Tell that mangy cur I'll find him one day, and when I do, he better cough up that damned jar of nectar he promised me.'*"

The Fae never forgot a promise. Larry grimaced, resigning himself to providing the gruff little Brownie a jar of nectar in his next incarnation ... or the one after that. Violet would eventually find him and demand the reward he had promised her for cleaning the office. It might be next year, or it could be a century from now, but the little Brownie would show up to collect, he was sure.

~

A QUESTION TEASED the edge of Larry's mind for a second, then it was gone. Jesse moved her ministrations from his side and stroked his head, her calloused hand gently playing with his ears. Larry gazed up at his soon-to-be former magical partner in silent thanks, then frowned and swiveled his gaze to Cerri. "But what happens to Jesse?"

Cerri's lips curved and her eyes sparkled with suppressed mirth. She gestured to Jesse and said, "You can tell him, if you'd like."

Jesse blushed and cleared her throat. Her gaze met Larry's, then skittered away. "Well, uh, it's like this, bud. Now that the SBI has arrested Litha, the Witch Council plans to appoint me as High Priestess of our old coven ... at the request of our former coven mates."

Larry gazed at his erstwhile magical partner in shock. "Whaaat?! Really? That's great news, Jess. We both know that job should have been yours, in the first place." He hesitated and added, "Uh, if you still want it, that is."

Jesse nodded, a slow grin parting her lips. "Yes, it's what I want, bud. It's what I've always wanted, really, but never quite felt ready for. But now, I think I am." She lowered her head to meet Larry's gaze directly, her eyes filled with loving warmth. "I'm ready, thanks to you, fur-face. You've taught me to trust myself—and to trust others, but verify. Always verify." She grinned down at him. "It's way past time for me to get off my duff and live life; I'm way too young to retire."

Larry turned his head and licked Jesse's hand as his former coven's rightful High Priestess leaned close and whispered in his ear. "Oh, and I'm moving the coven and its remaining members to San Antonio. There's a coven vacancy opening there soon and we all need a fresh start. Plus, I hear they have a great pizza place down there—and they deliver."

Larry chuckled softly, then closed his tired eyes one last time.

25

THE DEPARTMENT OF
ETERNAL ANIMAL FAMILIARS

Larry sensed movement and heard the echoes of many voices in a large space. This was the part he hated. The Department of Eternal Animal Familiars always reminded him of the Department of Motor Vehicles back on earth. Over the years, he had accompanied several of his former coven's witches to the DMV and the busy, impersonal space and rude, rushed staff always left him with an uncomfortable sense of déjà vu.

And now, here he was—back in Underworld's version of the DMV. Again. With an annoyed grunt, he shifted on the hard plastic chair. He may not have a corporeal body at the moment, but damn, these DEAF chairs still made his butt hurt, somehow.

A quiet sob to his left caught Larry's attention. With a heavy sigh, he sat up and opened his eyes. The ghostly form of a small cat not quite out of kitten-hood huddled in the chair next to his. The little Familiar retained the feline form of her previous life, just as he still had the ghostly body of a huge junkyard dog. Until they received their new physical forms, Familiars kept the shape, if not the substance, of their previous incarnation.

The little cat meowed sadly and gazed around the massive, open space, her eyes wide in terror. "What's happening? Why am I here?" She cried. "Where's Tiana? I want Tiana and a bowl of fresh tuna neoooooow!"

Larry stifled a groan. He hated to be the bearer of bad news, but someone had to explain things to the fearful little feline. "Listen cat ... what's your name?"

The kitten started, then turned her gaze to Larry and replied softly, "Um, I'm called Snowball. Do you know where Tiana is? I want to go home."

"Okay, um, Snowball," Larry replied, trying to keep his voice calm, but knowing his next words would scare her even more. "Here's the thing, kid. You're here, uh, because something bad must have happened to Tiana." When Snowball's eyes filled with tears, Larry hastily added a caveat. "Or maybe she got a promotion or something and doesn't need you anymore. Anyway, Tiana's no longer your magical partner. That's why you're here. Your DEAF caseworker will give you a new assignment, plus a spiffy new body, then you'll be sent back earth-side to partner with someone else."

"But I don't want to partner with anyone else," Snowball protested. "I like Tiana, and I like my job. She's an excellent potion witch, even though she's, like, really old—even for a witch. My job is to keep mice and bugs from getting into her potion room. It's easy and fun, and Tiana always gives me a reward for bringing her just the right dead mouse or bug to use in her magical brews." Her eyes widened dreamily. "I even have my own soft bed, but Tiana lets me sleep with her if I sneak under the covers quietly and don't move around too much. She even—"

A roaring snort interrupted Snowball's praise of her now former magical partner. "Doesn't matter how the old bat treated you, cat. She's gone and you're back here for another assignment, so stop whining and suck it up."

Larry leaned forward and spotted the speaker. An ancient ghostly badger crouched in the chair on the other side of Snowball. The badger's fur stuck up in all directions and his crusty grey nose quivered with indignation. Beady yellow eyes met Larry's. "Kids these days, I tell you. Back in my day, we didn't whine and complain when it was time for a new assignment. We just got on with things."

Suppressing a growl, Larry forced his voice to remain neutral. "She's new at this. It's probably her first incarnation change, so let's give her a break, okay?" He eyed the irate badger warily, hoping his rebuke was mild enough. Badgers had quick tempers and were scrappy fighters, so Larry really didn't want to provoke the creature. Familiars couldn't technically be injured while in their non-corporeal form, but a fight was a fight, and he just didn't have it in him right now. Not after the awful battle at the scrapyard. He purposefully pulled his mind from the violence and death he'd recently witnessed ... and experienced.

"Look, uh, Mr. Badger. I don't want to fight. Can we just agree to disagree and leave the kitten alone?" Larry just wanted to sit tight until his number was called. Then he could meet with his caseworker, try not to piss him off any more than usual, receive his next assignment and new body, and get the heck out of the Underworld.

After a discordant screech, a loudspeaker blared. "Number 136,789. Would number 136,789 report to the blue door. Now."

The badger heaved himself off his chair with an irritated wheeze. He glared at Larry and flicked a dismissive glance at Snowball, who was now pressed tightly against Larry's side. "Good thing they called my number, you scruffy hound. Otherwise, you and me would be having a right go 'round." With that parting shot, the badger shook his head in disgust and loped off across the large space before disappearing behind the requisite blue door.

"THANK YOU," said a small voice. "You didn't have to stick up for me like that, but I really appreciate it."

"It's okay." Larry shifted awkwardly, not used to random cuddling by his least favorite Familiar form. "Uh, can you ..." He gestured with his paw.

"Oh, sorry!" Snowball peeled herself off Larry's side and gracefully curled herself into the chair beside him. "When I get nervous, I cuddle. I'm a cuddler."

"That's ... great. But you might want to ask first," Larry replied kindly. "Not everyone likes unexpected cuddles."

Snowball took a moment to digest his words, then nodded sagely. "I understand. Ask first, then cuddle."

Larry suppressed a sigh. If there was anything he liked less than cats in general, it was kittens ... or any newbie Familiar or magical partner, for that matter. He was a powerful, centuries-old Familiar—one of the first ever created. He had been around the incarnation block way too many times; it was no wonder he was so jaded and cynical and had no desire to train a newbie magical partner. Who could blame him, right?

He hoped fervently that his new magical assignment would be to a relatively quiet life with an experienced magical partner who worked on boring magical things, like healing potions. He was determined to keep his big mouth shut long enough not to piss off his morose caseworker and wind up in a cat's body. Again.

Since he could do nothing but wait until his number was called ... which could be an hour or a week, Larry settled in and answered the kitten's many questions.

"Do Familiars always wind up back here for another assignment when their magical partner gets a promotion?" Snowball asked.

Larry knew the little cat's magical partner, a very elderly witch, had almost certainly died—as had Snowball's previous physical body, so this was a tough question to answer without crushing the poor thing's spirit. Since Snowball was such a young Familiar, she likely had a feline Familiar mother and had been born as a kitten on Earth, just like Midnight's kittens. Newbies. Yuck.

Larry's heart contracted when he thought of the vulnerable little kittens that the brave mama-cat had to leave behind when she and Ted escaped the scrapyard with the Universum. As the Felinus Universum, Midnight's Familiar form and her magical assignment were inextricably tied to Ted's family line and their onerous task of hiding the deadly machine their unscrupulous mage ancestor had created. It was their job to ensure the Universum didn't fall into the wrong hands and endanger the galaxy, and it had been a near thing this time.

Midnight had had no choice but to leave her kittens in Larry's care. She couldn't very well have taken them into hiding with her, exposing them to even greater dangers. Besides, while still very young, Midnight's kittens would soon be ready for their first Familiar assignment.

"WHAT ARE YOU THINKING ABOUT, Larry? You look sad. I don't want you to be sad." Snowball placed a tentative paw on Larry's side. "Would you like a cuddle?"

Larry shook off his melancholy musings. His idiotic act of heroism during the scrapyard battle had caused the loss of his physical body. Thus, he had failed in his task of protecting Midnight's kittens. He just hoped his demon friend Carb came through, as he'd promised, and taken the kittens to the animal shelter. Their magical partners would find the young feline Familiars there, he was sure.

"Uh, thanks, Snowball," Larry told the kitten. "I'm okay, and don't need a cuddle right now." His eyes widened as the youngling's eyes reflected acute disappointment. "Thanks so much for the offer, though. It's cheered me right up." He smiled gently down at the kindhearted feline.

Snowball reluctantly removed her paw from Larry's side and sighed. "If you don't want to answer my questions, I understand. Tiana always says ... said I talk too much."

Wracking his brain for Snowball's earlier question, Larry grimaced. So much had happened in the last twenty-four hours that he was almost certainly still in shock. *Oh, that's right.* Snowball had asked if Familiars always returned to DEAF for a new assignment, if their relationship ended with their current magical partner—for whatever reason.

"I don't mind answering your questions, Snowball. I just forgot what you asked for a moment there." Larry realized he needed to be diplomatic with his answer. He didn't want to set the young cat off on another crying jag. "Um, when a magical partner ... gets promoted, or no longer needs a magical Familiar for another reason, then a couple of things can happen. If the Familiar's physical form is still ... uh, in good shape, and there is a witch close by who needs a Familiar, sometimes DEAF will do an earth-side transfer, with no trip to the Underworld or new body needed."

Snowball's eyes narrowed as she considered Larry's answer. When sadness filled her eyes, he could tell the kitten had finally figured things out. She may be young, but this cat was really on the ball—now that she had gotten over the initial disorientation of suddenly finding herself in the supernatural world's version of the largest DMV in existence.

"What you're saying is that someone attacked Tiana and killed her, and my physical form was mortally injured while trying to defend her." Snowball's too knowing gaze met Larry's. "That is what you're saying, right? And that's why I'm here. I need a new body and a new magical partner because both ... are no more."

Larry sighed and nodded. "You're right, Snowball. That's exactly it. I'm so sorry."

"It's okay, I guess. I just wish Tiana had warned me this might happen. I was earth-born, so I've never had to go through this ... process." The little feline waved her paw at the massive, busy DEAF waiting area. She turned sympathetic eyes on Larry. "That's what happened to you, too, right? Your partner died and your physical form was kaput, as well."

Larry tilted his head, surprised at the young cat's easy acceptance. "Well, my magical partner didn't die, uh, like yours did, but yes, my physical body was badly injured during a fight and I ... it didn't make it. So that's why I'm here."

Curiosity lit Snowball's eyes. "So, you're just here for a new body, then? After you get one, you'll go back to your magical partner?"

With a regretful shake of his head, Larry replied, "I've been told I'm getting a new magical assignment, as well as a new body. Jesse—my previous magical partner, will have to do without a Familiar until DEAF assigns her a new one."

"Oh," the kitten stated, a tiny frown marring her sweet face. She studied Larry with big, questioning eyes. "But why?"

Larry wanted to roll his eyes so badly, but he didn't want to hurt the little cat's sensitive feelings, so he limited himself to a soft grunt. This was one reason he hated dealing with newbies —of either the Familiar or witchy sort; they asked soooo many questions. He got tired just thinking about it and whispered a prayer to the gods. *"To whoever is making these decisions ... please, don't assign me to a newbie magical partner. Pretty please."*

Faint feminine laughter answered Larry's plea. He peered around the room, not really expecting to see anyone laughing. Not surprisingly, every single Familiar seated in the acre of hard plastic chairs wore a dour expression. He shrugged in resignation; hardly anyone smiled or laughed in bureaucratic waiting rooms, whatever realm they were in.

"You don't have to answer me if you don't want," Snowball said, pulling Larry out of his dismal thoughts. Her whiskers drooped dejectedly. "I know I ask too many questions ... but how am I going to learn if I don't?" She protested.

Just as Larry opened his mouth to reply, the speaker squawked, echoing in the vast room. "Number 136,905, please report to the red door. That's 136,905 to the red door. Now." A shimmering ticket appeared in front of Larry, informing him the number just called belonged to him. He climbed down from his chair with a sinking feeling. The gods were laughing at him. He just knew it.

Larry gave Snowball a quick smile and said, "Good luck on your next assignment, kid." Then he padded reluctantly toward the red door, just knowing he would not like what he found behind it.

"Just, please, not a cat," he silently pleaded to whichever deity was listening. *"I'll be happy with almost any other animal body, and I won't even whine ... much ... about my new assignment, even if it's a with a magical newbie. Just, can we not do a cat body? Please and thank you."*

26

WHAT KIND OF A REWARD IS THIS?

Larry eased through the red door the guard held open for him, hoping against hope that his caseworker was taking another long vacation. Maybe his luck would hold, and he'd be able to sweet-talk an amenable temp, just like he did last time. Unfortunately, his gut told him he wouldn't be so lucky this time.

When he spotted Mort's ugly mug, surrounded by its flickering halo of green flames, peering through the glass on his office door, Larry knew neither luck nor the gods could help him this time. He would just have to keep his temper, watch his smart mouth, and hope for the best. Sigh.

Mort gestured with a clawed hand and opened his office door just enough to admit Larry, then scurried back behind his desk to sit in his fancy, cushioned executive chair. "Have a seat, Familiar," the demon growled, indicating the uncomfortable chair in front of his desk. It was one of the thousands of hard plastic client chairs that infested DEAF's headquarters—and most bureaucratic organizations in any realm.

From the mean glint in the demon's glowing red eyes, Larry

knew Mort hadn't been happy when he discovered a temp had given Larry a rocking Rottie-Pitt mix body for his last Familiar incarnation. He just hoped the poor temp had escaped with her life; he wouldn't put anything past Miserable Mort.

The demon lowered his gaze to his untidy desk and shuffled through several stacks of folders that rose almost as high as his head. Larry never ceased to be amazed the tall piles didn't tip over and scatter papers everywhere. Computers had never really caught on in the Underworld; the flowing rivers of death magic permeating the realm's air fried their circuits in no time.

"Ah, here it is," muttered Mort, expertly extracting a file from midway down one of the towering piles. He opened the folder and flipped casually through the papers within.

The demon's growing frown made Larry uneasy. Either his new assignment was soft as a peach, which would piss his case-worker off no end, or it was a high-profile one, which would also piss Mort off, since he knew Larry would receive accolades if he succeeded at an elite new assignment. Speaking of which, he had been very successful at his last job, hadn't he? He had even sacrificed his physical body to win the battle at the scrap-yard, thus earning enough time for Midnight and Ted to escape with the Universum, so the damn thing didn't fall into the wrong hands. He had helped save the galaxy, for the gods' sake. Surely, he was due a reward for that, wasn't he?

As if reading his mind, Mort tossed a small, round disc across his desk. He tapped the shiny golden disc with a claw and said, "This here is for you. Seems you ... ah, did a good job at your last assignment." The demon eyed Larry doubtfully, and muttered, "Somehow."

Larry swallowed a snarky retort and instead replied neutrally, "Thanks, Mort." He reached a paw toward the disc, which disappeared the moment he touched it. "I'll just take that for safekeeping, shall I?" Larry kept a small stash of valued items in a tiny pocket dimension that a former mage partner had gifted him centuries ago. He sent the disc there for safe-keeping before Mort could snatch it back. That disc represented a favor owed from the gods and would surely come in handy one day, when he got himself into more trouble than he could handle—which admittedly happened pretty regularly, so he had no hopes of hanging on to the damned thing for long. But still ... Mort wasn't having it back. Not yet anyway.

THE DEMON GROWLED IRRITABLY but didn't protest Larry's actions. It was the gods who awarded divine favor discs for services rendered above and beyond the call of duty, after all. Mort would need a very good reason to confiscate it, and Larry didn't plan on giving him one, if he could help it.

Larry attempted a friendly smile and asked, "So, what can you tell me about my next assignment?" He hadn't liked Mort's earlier frown when he had been reviewing his file, but the demon was now smiling slyly, which worried him even more. "It can't be that bad ... can it?" He asked, trying not to reveal his concern.

"Oh, it's bad, Familiar," Mort replied with a chuckle. "Knowing you as I do—and we've known each other for centuries, now, haven't we—you're not going to like your next assignment. At all."

Larry knew it was likely the irritating demon was simply baiting him, but his heart sank anyway. Hiding his worry behind a blandly inquisitive smile, he asked, "So, what do the gods ... I mean, you, have for me this time, Mort?" He despised the lazy, arrogant mid-level bureaucrat; the spiteful demon made Larry's incarnation transitions a misery every chance he got. Unable to help himself, Larry drawled, "Unlike your lazy ass, Mort, I'm always up for a challenge."

"You mean, you're always up to something, you little toe-rag," Mort snarled. The green flames flickering around the demon's head brightened, and he leaned forward, pinning Larry with a malevolent glare. "I don't know what the gods see in you, you piece of shi—"

"A sight more than they see in you, Mort," Larry shot back, regretting his words as soon as he uttered them. They were true, of course, but did he really have to piss off the demon in charge of assigning his next physical form every time they met? Well, shit.

A slow, malicious grin exposed Mort's razor-sharp teeth. He tapped the folder in front of him meaningfully. "I may not be able to prevent you from getting this assignment, Familiar, but I can make damn sure your physical body leaves a lot to be desired while you're performing it."

With that, the fire demon vanished in a puff of green flames. Simultaneously, a sharp tug in Larry's core informed him that Mort had assigned his next physical form before disappearing. His new body wouldn't be revealed until Larry began his new assignment, but he was certain that he really wasn't going to like it. Not one bit. Closing his eyes with a sigh, he prayed in vain to whoever was listening. *"Just ... not a cat. Please."*

Larry knew that his caseworker's disappearance meant his next mission was top secret. Mort obviously didn't have a high enough security clearance to know exactly what Larry's next assignment involved, which was what had pissed the flame demon off so much. Larry shifted in the hard chair, trying to get comfortable. One of the DEAF higher ups would soon be along to brief him, he was sure.

As if he had any hope of influencing the coming course of events, Larry closed his eyes and whispered, *"Just, please, not a cat, not a cat, not a cat,"* until a rich, feminine laugh behind him interrupted his wishful chanting.

Twisting in his chair, he opened his eyes to a vision of divine loveliness. The goddess Hecate lounged on a low leather couch positioned against the office's far wall. He had only met this goddess in person once before, but he knew what was expected of him when faced with a divine being. He immediately jumped off his chair and bowed low. "Well met, goddess Hecate. It is a great pleasure to see you again."

The goddess snickered, her crimson-red lips curving in a smug smile. Long, elegant fingers played with a strand of gleaming ebony curls, while amusement gleamed in the ancient goddess's dark eyes. "Oh, drop the act, Familiar. You know as well as I do that, when a goddess takes an interest in you, it's almost never a pleasure."

Larry stifled a groan and padded over to sit at attention on the thin rug in front of the couch, heart pounding with fear. Whatever interest the powerful goddess had in him would surely bring great peril. Still, after the tragic events of his last incarnation, Larry was deeply committed to listening to his gut feelings. Those feelings told him that, while Hecate had a divinely dangerous assignment for him, she didn't actively mean him harm. In fact, the worry lurking in her dark eyes indicated she had grave concerns about his next assignment, as well.

With a resigned sigh, Larry asked the all-important question. "You have a magical newbie for me to train, don't you? Judging by your demeanor, whoever it is will be a magical powerhouse, once their powers manifest." He eyed the lovely Greek goddess speculatively. "And I imagine this person has an important task or two they must successfully complete, or ...."

"Or the Earth and all the realms will soon be leveled under a tidal wave of divine destruction," Hecate stated flatly. The goddess gave Larry a thin smile. "Your new magical partner is the only one who can stop the coming chaos, Familiar. Your job is to prepare her for her new role and to support her once she occupies it."

Larry wanted to ask, 'Why me?' But he already knew the answer to that question. He was a first-generation Familiar— one of the oldest and most powerful Familiars in existence. He had saved the gods' bacon more than once over the centuries, and his heroic actions during this last assignment had even helped save the damned galaxy. Whenever the gods feared a world-shattering event, and needed a powerful magical team to help prevent it, Larry knew he was at the top of their list of Familiars to be assigned to help deal with the crisis. Sigh.

HECATE AND LARRY talked for several long hours about his new assignment, then the goddess bound Larry to an oath of silence. Most of what they had discussed must remain confidential for the time being. All Larry could say, if asked, was that his new magical partner had no idea about the supernatural world yet, and that it was his job to help her find her way once she discovered her supernatural heritage. That was it.

At the end of their conversation, the two sat in silence for a time, the importance of coming events weighing heavily on both their minds. Finally, Hecate leaned forward and studied Larry's non-corporeal form closely. Then she grinned widely, a wicked glint of amusement in her eyes.

Eyes narrowing in suspicion, Larry asked, "You can see what my next physical form is going to be, can't you? Will you tell me?" Hope surged, and he begged the goddess for a favor. "Look, this next assignment is gonna be a tough one, agreed? Plus, I aced my last job, right? I mean, the galaxy is still in one piece—and I helped keep it that way."

He huffed a frustrated growl. "I'm willing to bet that Mort

the Moron has assigned me the body of a mouse, or a toad, or something similarly unimpressive. That fire demon hates me." Giving the goddess a pleading look, he whined, "I can't do this job properly if everyone thinks I'm a laughingstock of a Familiar. Can you change Mort's body choice? Please?"

Hecate's brows rose, and she fixed Larry with a questioning gaze. "Are you calling in your divine favor, Familiar?" She held out her hand and made gimme fingers. "If so, please hand over the disc you just earned, and I'll grant your boon."

Larry studied the goddess intently. Her dark eyes carried a warning and his gut agreed with it. Now was not the time to redeem his divine favor, especially just because he didn't want to live his next life as a damn parakeet or dormouse. He knew his magic would be just as powerful, no matter his physical form. With a sigh, Larry accepted the lessons he'd learned during his last assignment and listened to his gut feeling.

"Nope, I'm not calling in my divine favor just yet, thanks," he told Hecate with a firm shake of his head. "I get the feeling I should save it for something really important."

Hecate withdrew her hand, her expression registering warm approval. She nodded sagely, a small smile hovering on her lips. "It seems you have learned the wisdom of trusting in yourself ... and in those around you, during your last incarnation, Familiar. Those skills will stand you in good stead during your next assignment, I'm sure."

Larry's ears perked. A compliment from a goddess was nothing to be sneezed at. He scrambled to his feet when Hecate rose and started gathering her things. Giving the goddess a hasty bow, he repeated his earlier request. "So, your, uh, Highness ... goddess ... can you please tell me what physical form I'll have for my upcoming assignment?"

Hecate merely snickered and shook her head, her last words drifting over her shoulder as she strode out of the room. "I think not, Familiar. It's probably best if you discover that for yourself." Laughter heralded the goddess's exit, just as it had announced her entrance several hours earlier.

Well, damn, Larry mused. *At least I tried.* With a heartfelt sigh, he padded after the goddess, knowing he would discover what his new Familiar form would be soon enough. And that he definitely wasn't going to like it. *Sigh.*

EPILOGUE

Surprise at the Shelter

Larry woke up to a riot of incessant barking. Clangs and bangs and human voices echoed in the distance. Still groggy from his transition back to Earth, he opened his eyes and gazed around the small enclosure.

In the dim light, all he could make out was that a high concrete wall made up three sides of the room, while the fourth featured a tall chain-link gate. The floor was bare concrete, its chill steadily seeping through the thin blanket underneath his body.

He closed his eyes as a wave of nausea coursed through him. Underworld to Earth transitions were always tough.

Dread made his heart race when he recalled his earlier conversation with Hecate—and the amused gleam in her eyes when she departed. The goddess had refused to tell him what physical form his Familiar spirit would inhabit during its next incarnation.

Vaguely, he remembered pissing Mort, his vindictive DEAF caseworker, all the way off. Yet again. *Sigh.* He just couldn't keep his damned mouth shut for anything, could he?

Closing his eyes, Larry dozed off again. The transition had completely exhausted him, as it usually did. He would discover his new Familiar form soon enough, but for now, he needed a nap.

SOMETIME LATER, lights clicked on in the hallway outside his cell. He blinked and squinted his eyes, temporarily blinded by the bright light. His sensitive ears picked up the low hum of the florescent bulbs. Whatever physical body he had, it came with excellent hearing, at least.

With a resigned sigh, Larry rose to his feet. *Good ... at least I'm on four legs,* he mused muzzily. At least I'm not a damned bird. But that didn't eliminate the worst possibility. *Not a cat. Please, not a cat.*

Larry repeated the 'not a cat' mantra as he padded over to a dented metal bowl in the corner. Once his eyes adjusted to the light, he should be able to see his reflection in the bowl's reflective surface. Eyes widening, he stared down at his new face and snorted in disgust. *Well, shit.* Not a cat, but almost as bad. Okay, definitely as bad. Worse, even.

Larry snarled at the fluffy horror staring back at him from the bottom of the bowl. Did he really have to back-talk his case manager at DEAF? Again? He and Mort had shared a mutually antagonistic relationship for centuries ... and boy, did that damned fire demon know how to get even.

Peering back at Larry from the bottom of the shiny metal bowl was a small poodle sporting a long, well-shaved muzzle, a moist black nose, lots of fluffy white fur ... and incredibly bright pink ears. *Holy moly.* He really needed to practice keeping his mouth shut. *Sigh*

He had learned a lot during his last Familiar gig, including not to be so cynical and detached and to trust his gut and those he worked with, especially his magical partner. But he sure as heck hadn't learned how to keep his big snarky mouth shut—not that he ever would, Larry wryly admitted to himself.

With a resigned sigh, Larry lapped at the clear water in the bowl, drinking his fill. Transitioning always made him thirsty.

At least I'm not a cat, he brooded. But still ... who the hell would take him seriously in this prissy poodle form? He was one of the oldest and most powerful magical Familiars ever to exist. And he looked like he should be performing in a circus or poking his head out of some rich lady's purse. *Crapola.*

He was very grateful to have lived the last century as a handsome and huge hunk of a canine. He'd just have to power through his new Familiar gig in this floofy pink-eared poodle body. He didn't have much of a choice.

Larry considered filing a grievance against his caseworker with DEAF, but that could make things worse. He'd wind up as a damned toad or newt if he wasn't careful. Shuddering, he remembered the fiasco several centuries before, when he'd mouthed off to Mort and wound up as a cat for his next assignment. He'd hated that Familiar gig as a cat—especially one assigned to a witch during the Burning Times. Talk about true suckage.

At least he had been given a dog form for this incarnation. *So, yeah ... at least not a cat. Yay.*

~

SPEAKING OF CATS, Larry heard faint meows coming from somewhere down the long hallway and recognized the feline cries. Carb had come through; Midnight's kittens were safe at the shelter until their new magical partners came to collect them. And at least he knew where was: Furry Friends Animal Rescue—also known as pet prison, he morosely amended.

Vowing to work on accepting his new Familiar form, Larry shrugged and shook his head, his long pink ears flapping as he did.

In his mind, he was still a rough, tough junk-yard dog. He'd just have to make sure his newbie magical partner learned that, while he may look like a pretty pink boy on the outside, he had the heart of a 'real' dog on the inside.

A LOW, feminine voice startled Larry from his dismal musings. "Oh, my god! You're just adorable! Look at those pink ears on you! And the pink tail, too. What happened to bring you in here, you little cutie?"

Larry tried hard not to roll his eyes. *So, my freaking tail is pink, too,* he brooded. Resigning himself to his new reality, he plastered on a doggie smile and regarded his new magical partner with interest.

The woman was attractive, with long, black hair, tanned olive skin, and big, green eyes set above high cheekbones. Her full lips curved in a kind smile, and her eyes sparkled with delighted amusement.

She studied the clipboard attached to his cage. "It says here you were picked up as a stray almost a week ago. Hmmm." Brows lowered, she frowned down at Larry and shrugged. "But look at you. You're the prettiest puppers, and so beautifully groomed. It's hard to believe your human mom or dad aren't looking for you, sweetie."

Larry wagged his tail at the woman's words, but worry niggled at him. If he had been here for almost a week, why couldn't he remember anything until now?

Almost as if she could hear Larry's concern, the woman read the form's intake notes aloud. "It says here you were asleep when the animal control officer found you and you've been sleeping ever since. The vet notes say there's nothing wrong with you and to just let you sleep."

Her eyes softened in sympathy. "I've heard that stray dogs are often so exhausted from their ordeal that, once rescued, they sometimes sleep for days. I'm soooo sorry for whatever happened to bring you here, bud."

Not knowing what to do with the woman's empathy, Larry simply sat on his haunches and eyed her with confusion. This couldn't possibly be his next magical partner, could it? She was too pretty, too young (possibly late twenties), and way too non-magical.

Curious, he activated his magical powers and looked beyond the woman's innocuous surface appearance. What he found shocked him to the core. This human-seeming woman packed more magical power, locked away deep inside her, than almost any supernatural creature he'd ever met—and, over the centuries of his long life, he'd met a lot of supernaturals.

A deep, burning anger brewed inside him. The poor thing's magic was hidden behind so many locked metaphysical doors and memory blockers that he feared the results when those barriers broke open, as they eventually would.

MOVEMENT outside his cell ended Larry's silent musings. The woman had seated herself seated directly on the cold concrete floor in front of his kennel, and was still studying the clipboard in her hand.

"My name is Alex, by the way, pup," she murmured absently. Then she looked up from her reading and smiled thoughtfully at him. "It says here that the tag on your collar when they brought you in had nothing more than a name ... Larry."

She grinned widely, her luminous green eyes sparkling with delight. "And it says you're a boy, despite the pink ears and tail!"

Larry sneezed irritably and rolled his eyes, then remembered his manners and his upcoming mission. Opening his muzzle in a doggie grin, he smiled toothily at his soon-to-be-new magical partner ... Alex, she said her name was. It wasn't her fault that his asshole of a case manager had gotten the last laugh by giving Larry the most ridiculous physical form he could think of.

Despair threatened to overtake Larry when he recalled Hecate's warnings regarding the difficulties and dangers he and Alex would soon face. A magical newbie with bound powers and her small, fluffy poodle Familiar ... how would anyone in the supernatural community take them seriously?

Larry vowed not to give in to his worries. It was his job to do the best he could to train and support his newbie magical partner, so that was what he would do, no matter what.

He brightened when it occurred to him that, once Alex's magic was unbound, she would have more power in her pinkie finger than most supernaturals. Plus, his laughable physical form provided him with the advantage of surprise; no one would ever believe this farcical body contained one of the most powerful magical Familiars ever created.

Huh. Maybe Hecate was right to put her faith in them, after all. Alex would be a formidable magical force once Larry helped her unbind her magic and learn how to use it. And the bad guys would never suspect Alex's prissy poodle Familiar could easily magically wipe the floor with them. *What do you know? Maybe Mort the Moron had done him a favor, after all.*

∽

"...WELL, LARRY, WHAT DO YOU THINK?" Alex gazed at Larry inquiringly, her eyes reflecting an eager nervousness.

Larry realized with a start that she must have been talking to him for a while—and he hadn't been listening. *Darn it.*

He stood and padded closer to the chain-link gate, tilting his head in the universal non-verbal sign for *'can you please repeat that?'* While he had the ability to speak to Alex, either out loud or mind-to-mind, it was probably better she didn't know that. Yet.

Alex huffed a laugh. "You are the thinkingest dog I've ever met. If I didn't know better, I'd say you've been lost in deep thought for the last five minutes, and not just totally ignoring me."

If only you knew, Larry mused. He fixed his dark, almond-shaped eyes on the kind woman, then gave a soft woof and let his ears and tail droop dejectedly. His canine behavior elicited the response he expected.

"Ohhh, you poor thing!" Alex murmured softly. "You've had a heck of a week, haven't you? Abandoned outside in the cold, no owner coming to claim you ... no wonder you're so out of it."

She leaned forward, her eyes intent on his. "What I asked was if you'd like to come home and live with me, Larry. I volunteer here at the shelter on weekends, and it's made me want a dog of my own." She rolled her eyes and huffed a laugh. "Of course, I envisioned something quite a bit larger and ... um, not nearly as cute as you are. But I think we have a connection here, right?"

Remembering the hard-earned lessons of his past incarnation, Larry silently repeated his new mantras. *Trust in yourself. Listen to your gut. Practice teamwork.*

He wagged his tail and grinned a wide doggie smile, then slipped his paw through the cage door. The magical Familiar bond snapped firmly into place when Alex wrapped Larry's paw gently in her hand.

WANT to read about Alex's adventures with Larry, her snarky new magical Familiar? Receive a free sample of Hecate's Heir, Book One in the Crossroads Keeper series, by joining my VIP Reader's Club. Club members also have exclusive access to bonus scenes, monthly book fairs, discounts, and more.

For more information and purchase links, visit my website: **www.samanthablackwoodnovelist.com**

READER'S NOTE: This prequel features Larry's origin story, told from his perspective. The rest of the books in this series are told from Alex's perspective, although Larry certainly has a say, too. Just you try keeping that dog quiet, lol.

Barghest shifter, plus a posse full of quirky supernaturals, Alex takes the fight to the Underworld, where she and her team must defeat a dark goddess and end her plans for world chaos.

Mythical Greek gods, quirky supernatural creatures, a newbie Crossroads Keeper, and her sassy, snarky ... and magical pink-eared poodle sidekick battle the forces of chaos in this urban fantasy series filled with adventure and humor, along with a smidge of romance and newfound family ties.

Visit my website to join my VIP Reader's Club newsletter and receive your free sample of Hecate's Heir and for purchase links to this and other books in the Crossroads Keeper series.

www.samanthablackwoodnovelist.com

ALSO BY SAMANTHA BLACKWOOD

The Crossroads Keeper Series

Prequel - Larry's Familiar Tale

Book 1 - Hecate's Heir

Book 2 - Persephone's Problem

Book 3 - Demeter's Dilemma

Book 4 - Hades in Hot Water - Coming Soon

Book 5 - The Chaos Council - Coming Soon

Book 6 - Nixing Nyx

The Kitchen Witchery Series

Book 1 - The Maple Muffin Murder

Book 2 - The Lemon Croissant Corpse

Book 3 - The Damson Danish Death - Coming Soon

For purchase links, please visit my website.

www.samanthablackwoodnovelist.com

Join my VIP Reader's Club to receive a free sample of Hecate's Heir and to receive email news about upcoming releases, bonus content, Larry's Life Blog, discounts, and more.

For more information or to sign up for my VIP Reader's Club newsletter, please visit my website:

www.samanthablackwoodnovelist.com

ABOUT THE AUTHOR

Samantha Blackwood writes novels and series in the urban fantasy, supernatural, and paranormal cozy mystery genres.

She lives near the beach in sunny Portugal with her husband and their pack of rescue dogs. She worked professionally with dogs for most of her life and proudly claims the title of 'Crazy Dog Lady.' Her friends and family don't disagree...

Of course, she couldn't imagine not including dogs in her writing, so there's at least one sassy, snarky canine character, based on one of her own dogs, in each of her books.

She has a lot of fun giving her fictionalized fur-kids magical abilities—and voices. We all know dogs don't really need human words to communicate, but it's nice—and hilarious—to hear them tell us exactly what they think!

For more information, please contact the author.
Website: www.samanthablackwoodnovelist.com
E-mail: sam@samanthablackwoodnovelist.com

Find her on social media.
Facebook.com/samanthablackwoodnovelist
Instagram.com/samanthablackwoodnovelist
Pinterest.com/samanthablackwoodnovelist